PRELUDE TO WAR

He hit the Sioux warrior so crushingly that he drew only a grunt. For the moment Sam felt his knees against the earth on each side of the Sioux, his crotch pressing down on the warrior's backbone. He hammered him back of the ear with the barrel of his Colt.

Sam waited for another warrior to jump him. And then, above the pounding of hoofs and the snap and rattle of iron and wood and leather, he heard the clear, piercing scream of a woman.

We will send you a free catalog on request. Any titles not in your local book store can be purchased by mail. Send the price of the book plus 50¢ shipping charge to Tower Books, P. O. Box 270, Norwalk, Connecticut 06852

Titles currently in print are available for industrial and sales promotion at reduced rates. Address inquiries to Tower Publications, Inc., Two Park Avenue, New York, New York 10016, Attention: Premium Sales Department.

ENEMY IN SIGHT

Bill Bragg

TOWER BOOKS NEW YORK CITY

A TOWER BOOK

Published by

Tower Publications, Inc.
Two Park Avenue
New York, N.Y. 10016

Copyright ©1980 by Tower Publications, Inc.

All rights reserved
Printed in the United States

CHAPTER 1

Three hairy men in dingy buckskin slipped silently through the lodge-pole pine timber. The last man in line led the shaggy saddle horses. On their back trail, well concealed in thicker timber, they had tied up the string of pack ponies laden with their spring catch of beaver pelts. Although they moved as noiselessly as their shadows, Singin' Sam Sling advanced too boldly for the comfort of his comrades.

The scrawny old man with the ragged beard, piloting the horses, grabbed Sam's arm when they checked into a green mountain park for a breather. "You'll lose your hair sure, Sam, if yuh don't slow down. I can smell Sioux bucks plain as all git out."

Sam twitched his long sunburnt nose savoring the air. He wore a youthful look despite the deep lines in his gaunt brown face, and the coarse black hair that fell to his greasy collar.

"I smell smoke," he replied. "What wind there is comes from the direction of our winter camp. Shorty, maybe Buffalo Hump and his squaw need help right bad."

"If a Sioux war party jumped our camp," Shorty

argued, "time's long past to help Hump and the Night Star. Better for us to go slow and see what started the smoke down thar."

The third man of the party, a short Indian, was squatting on lean hams, peering through a break in the timber that offered a view of the quiet beaver meadow just below the pines.

"What you think, Tom?" Sam asked. "We spotted that smoke from up on the divide this mornin'. You figure we're goin' too slow? Night Star's your sister. A pretty squaw worth savin' from those Sioux war whoops."

Tom Bear Mouth shook his head. "Smoke look bad," he answered in his broken Agency English. "But can't see yet where come from."

"Let's git to where we can see," Sam said impatiently.

"Go fast, Sioux see us first, they there," argued Tom.

"But think of your sister, Tom. Maybe she's holed up in the shack or around the cache along with Hump, just prayin' for us to come fast."

"We see smoke long time now. Too late for pray if Sioux down there."

Rocky Mountain Shorty Gadberry, chewing tobacco, minding the ponies so they wouldn't snort or whinny, broke in to the pow wow. "You're too hot-livered, Sam. You go bustin' along like a blind hawg in a root cellar, and shore as all git out, them Sioux'll make bridle tassels out'n your hair. Anyway, it's not a cinch bet that smoke's comin' from our winter camp. Might be somethin' else in the woods. We work along easy through this timber, and right quick we'll git to whar we can look things over a hull lot. If Sioux bucks is tryin' to hide out, we'll see 'em soon as they spot us.

Maybe sooner. And if so," he slapped the barrel of his heavy Sharps buffalo gun," Susy, here, 'ull git in the first lick."

"Ain't been a thunder and lightnin' storm all this June to start a fire," said Sam. "Smoke don't come from no cook fire built by Night Star. She's too smart to use wood that makes smoke. She'd do her cookin' with quakin' asp. So leavin' out lightnin', somebody built the fire that raised that smoke down there. And it's my belief that somebody was a bunch of Sioux raidin' our winter camp."

Sam Sling knew well enough his two friends were offering sane counsel but a heavy feeling of guilt had oppressed him since dawn when the smoke had first been seen. The trappers had gone to the high country leaving Buffalo Hump and his wife in charge of the camp, presumably well hidden in a patch of quakers with the cache filled with the fall take of beaver pelts. The trapping party had planned for a stay of three weeks away from camp but had cut short the work, gathered traps and furs, packed horses, and headed down country upon seeing the thin streamer of smoke.

Sam's feeling of guilt came from the fact that he had led the party into this timbered country in the southern part of the Big Horn mountains the fall before. Mountain streams, of late years, had been trapped out, but he had heard of one secluded stream where white men had not set out a single trap. Trouble was that this country lay within territory set aside for the Sioux tribes by federal treaty. Even though General Custer had reported discoveries of gold in the Black Hills, army troops continued to bar out white settlers from the vast land north of the North Platte, bounded by the Big Horns on the west, and the Black Hills to the east. The Bozeman Trail to the Montana gold fields had been blocked. The Indians had even burned down the hated forts, C.F. Smith and Phil Kearny.

But Tom Bear Mouth, Buffalo Hump, and the Night Star were from the Shoshone tribe now camped far west in the Wind River country. Enmity over hunting territory ran between the Sioux and the Shoshones. The latter tribe also laid claim to the area where Sam had found a beaver bonanza. It had not been difficult to persuade the Indians to come along on the expedition. Rocky Mountain Shorty had been more cautious but he had at last given in to Sam's coaxing since the two whites had been trapping and hunting partners for the past four years from the Canadian line to the Mexican border.

"I can't take it so slow," Sam said. "I just got to find out what's happened." He walked over to his blaze-faced, buckskin pony, Baldy. He took the bridle reins from Shorty's hand, and reached for a stirrup. His Henry .44 caliber magazine rifle was in its saddle boot. His Colt six-gun, chambered to take similar size shells, hung from his belt.

Tom Bear Mouth shook his head and muttered, "White brave." Sam understood that in the Indian's opinion, he was foolhardy.

Shorty worked his whiskered jaws on his tobacco, watching his partner mount Baldy. He made no offer to board his own pony and follow Sam's lead.

"By Cracklin!," he declared. "I don't know what yuh aim to do, gallivantin' around on a hoss in this timber, but me and Tom'll foller along slow. If we hear shootin' we'll try to figure out somethin'. But don't count too much on us. Might be a hull pack of Sioux down thar."

Sam knew Shorty and Tom were brave enough, but being uncertain as to the size of the Sioux war party, he would not run undue risk before they could gain plenty of information. They were frontier veterans. They had fought the Sioux before and they held no illusions—as did some of the greenhorn soldiers manning the Powder River country outposts—that one white man could whip ten Indians.

"Somehow or other, if I think they're hid out down there," said Sam, "I'll try and get a count on 'em."

"Maybe they already took tally on us and have built that smoke to drag us into a trap," Shorty said. "If they have got the Hump and Night Star, maybe they know we're still somewhere in these hills, and they're tryin' to wipe us all out."

"It's a mile down to camp." Sam kicked Baldy in the ribs with moccasined heels. "I can't walk fast as this cayuse where timber's thick. Keep your eyes and ears open. If you decide things have gone wrong for me and the others, pull your freight out'n the mountains."

They parted without shaking hands. Frontier partners were not long on sentiment. All Shorty said, as Sam rode away was, "Keep your hair on straight, bub."

Sam trusted his pony for Baldy was a prized hunting horse, broken to stand under gunfire when buffalo kills were made by the partners, or skirmishes waged with roving Indians. Baldy would even pack a freshly killed grizzly bear pelt back of the saddle, which, Sam knew, was about top performance for a pony.

Sam's problem was to reach a position where he could scout out the location of the winter camp in its quaking asp patch. The timber thinned out along this lower flank. As he rode along, with Baldy picking his way carefully through raspberry brush and around the mossy green down logs like a well trained bird dog, Sam caught occasional glimpses of the beaver meadow to his left. It was a quiet green bowl, fragrant with early June grass and moist along a clear trout stream, starred with the yellow of buttercups and the blue of mountain daisies.

Gentle slopes fingered down from the timber to the meadow. But Sam knew that he had to break into the open and work his way far down one of these pitches before he could set eye on the camp hideout. Willow brush grew thickly along the stream, offering good concealment if Sioux warriors had raided the camp then hidden out to ambush the three trappers.

Sam knew that so far as they were able, Shorty and Tom would be following slowly along his trail, straining their eyes at every step to discover his whereabouts or signs of the Indians.

If it hadn't been that he blamed himself for bringing the Hump and his pretty Indian wife into these lonely mountains, Sam would not have started this bold ride against unknown odds. He knew also that if disaster had overtaken the expedition, no aid could be secured from the nearest army post of Cantonment Sparks, far to the east on a fork of the North Platte River.

Sam and Shorty were outside the law, taking beaver on Sioux treaty land. The three Shoshones might have believed they possessed a justifiable trapping right up here but Shoshone claims to this particular section had not been allowed by the treaty. If the Sioux had killed Buffalo Hump and Night Star, they would not be outside the law so far as the army was concerned.

When Sam thought of the army, and its regulations against frontiersmen, he snorted angrily, remembering his own enlistment which had ended with an honorable discharge four years before down at Fort Fred Steele. His brother Rick, an infantry sergeant of long service, had induced his younger brother to enlist at the close of the war between the states. Sam had come west with his brother's regiment, but irked by regulations, he had taken his discharge after his first hitch.

Sam and Rocky Mountain Shorty, like many of their mountain brethren, considered the treaty line had been drawn for the breaking. They would risk their hair whenever chances for a good kill of buffalo or catch of beaver seemed good. They respected the fighting qualities of the Sioux and Cheyennes in the Powder River country but asserted the army had made pets of the Indians who had been hostiles a few years before and taken many a scalp from walkaheap and whoa-haw soldiers up around Forts Kearny and Smith. Tough men like the two trappers might be taming the frontier of Wyoming Territory for oncoming civilization, but they didn't think of it that way. They hated civilization as heartily as they did the Sioux. They liked the free life of the west and they would go where they pleased in plains and mountains, and dare the Sioux or the soldiers to check them.

As Baldy nosed along, Sam kept an eye peeled to his left flank where occasional openings in the timber gave him a good view of the beaver meadow. The sun was almost noon high, and the valley slept peacefully under the balmy June sky. Once he saw a doe across the stream, feeding along the edges of blue timber. She sighted the lanky frontiersman on the buckskin pony and pricked up her mule-like ears. Sam decided that she had fawns hidden nearby. She was thin enough to be a mother. If the doe was hiding her young out so near the camp, then it didn't appear likely to Sam that Indians would be around. But then, the Sioux might have made their raid and gone into hiding long before the doe led her young out of the timber.

He had told Shorty and Tom Bear Mouth that he would get a count on the Sioux. But just how to achieve this without losing his scalp was something to give a man pause for thought. If he rode out boldly, they might pepper him with buffalo arrows, or dump him with a load of slugs from an old trade musket.

But if he didn't make a break pretty soon, he wouldn't get a good look toward the camp or know for certain that Sioux had raided it.

He wasn't more than fifty yards above the quaker patch where the winter shack had been built. The wind was light and warm but it was blowing straight toward Sam. It was rank with the smell of smoke.

Dismounting, he dropped the ends of his reins to the earth. His pony was trained to stand without being tied by the head. He drew the Henry from its rawhide sheath and carefully checked for action and full magazine. Old Shorty swore by Susy, his single-shot .50 caliber buffalo gun. It wasn't filled up with new-fangled machinery like a repeater that would jam up and let a man down in a pinch. Shorty could knock over a buffalo bull at six hundred yards with his Sharps. But Sam had a high respect for the Henry and the Colt hand gun.

He edged from the timber, hiding in brush and shadows cast by the tall pines wherever cover was offered. He felt quite certain that if Sioux were hidden out in the beaver meadow, they had long since spotted him moving down country. He was running at chances to get to a place where he could see the camp location. A scantily timbered point, stretching down toward the creek, obscured his vision. He had to get low enough to see around the trees.

The smell of the smoke informed his nose that more than wood had been set afire. Under Shorty's teaching, Sam had schooled his eyes, ears and nose for the frontier. Wood smoke smelled different than the smoke from burning cloth or blankets. Sam could smell a distinct odor of burnt cloth on the wind.

He came out to where cover was no longer possible. He estimated that he was about a hundred long horse jumps from a brush bend of the creek. The willows grew thickly enough there to hide twenty or thirty men and horses. The brush was ribboned with narrow trails trodden by browsing deer and elk. Skilled riders could move around in it under hiding.

This bright land, as a general rule in spring, rang to the songs of little mountain birds that loved the grass and the streams. Song birds were not sounding off today. Instead, as Sam finally reached a point where he could take a gander at the spot in the slope where they had dug the beaver cache, a flock of large black and white birds flapped off across the meadows squawking harshly.

They were magpies and meateaters. Something around the cache or the camp in the quakers had aroused them. Then Sam had appeared, frightening them. They were warning the wilderness.

Sam's heart missed a beat. From the corner of his eye, he saw a black hole in the grassy slope where the beaver cache had been dug. That wasn't all he saw in that brief glance. Something warm and brown, something that resembled a naked human leg, protruded from the cache. The flesh gleamed under the June sun.

The time was past now for Sam Sling to hide out and ponder and wonder if the Sioux were down in the willows. Tom Bear Mouth had called him "White Brave." He knew that his impulsive nature had gained him a reputation, even among enemy Indians, of foolhardiness. He was also a man of imagination, a sort of rude frontier bard. It had long been his custom to waste the dreary hours in winter camps, singing frontier ballads or, when his repertoire ran thin, composing his own verses to familiar music. The Shoshones knew all about his singing, for all Indians liked music. Quite likely the Sioux also had heard about Singin' Sam Sling, as Indian gossip ran over the plains and mountains like pale-face chatter in a New England village.

Sam wanted to draw the Indians from the brush. These Sioux were proud men. He whipped up the Henry and cracked a couple of slugs into the brush. He began to sing his own song as he advanced slowly down the slope on his knee-high moccasins stained with beaver blood and horse sweat.

> Oh take me back to the buff'ler days
> When Injuns whooped in the prairie haze
> Deadwood gold shined in the pan,
> The range was free to every man.

That last line referred to Sam's contempt for army regulations on trespassing treaty lands. When his hoarse song had wound up, he began to taunt the Sioux, telling them they were women who preferred to hide in the brush rather than come out and fight a long hair. He advised them to go back to camp and help the squaws gather wood and water. They could send out the little boys of the tribe to do their fighting. He punctuated his jeering talk with snapping bullets. Sam broke down Sioux patience. They broke from cover, a dozen naked painted men on hard-running ponies. He stood his ground, the Henry held ready for a target. The leading buck, riding a yellow pony, pulled a bow string to his ear and drove an arrow through the slack of Sam's shirt, penetrating the flat skin of his belt line.

CHAPTER 2

In a jam like this one, a man couldn't waste time pulling out an arrow head. The ground shook to the soft thunder of the scampering unshod hoofs. Singin' Sam, dropping to one knee, counted a dozen wild riders in the line of horsemen. He could see the red, green, and black war paint on the faces and bodies of the warriors. They charged straight up the gently rising slope, bending and swaying to throw the long hair who faced them off his line of aim.

The brave who had shot Sam with the arrow galloped a half dozen paces in the lead. He was naked except for paint and breech cloth. He had fastened a bunch of feathers and a war medicine bag of otter skin to the streaming black tail of his yellow pony. Squinting his eyes against the sun glare, Sam decided this buck was a war chief and the most likely target for the Henry.

The arrow wound was burning. The shaft, sticking out of his flapping buckskin shirt, hampered Sam's movements. He hoped that Shorty and Tom Bear Mouth were somewhere up in the timber, near enough by now, to get a count on the strength of the war party.

Sam figured he had done his good deed for the day. He had taunted the Sioux into exposing their strength. They had carefully set their trap but Sam had sprung it prematurely with his buffalo song and taunts about Sioux courage.

He felt a bit nervy as he waited for the ponies to come near enough so that he could see the white rims of their walled eyes. Many a greenhorn had lost his hair while adventuring across the Great Plains, by emptying his rifle before the foe had come within good shooting distance.

The Sioux were barking out their wolfish war whoops as they rode. The shrill echoes and the cracks of the few guns carried by the warriors, rang back from the rocky rims of the valley. Even if Shorty and Tom couldn't see, they could hear the fight. Whether they would pull out of the hills immediately or come to Sam's aid was a question that Sam had no time now to worry about.

He ran a good chance of losing his hair in this pretty little mountain meadow where he had spent a passable winter in fairly comfortable quarters, fleshing and stretching a good stake in fur.

It was amazing, he reflected, how much a man could think about in the short space of time that had been given him since he jumped the Sioux and they snapped an arrow into the meat over his short ribs. If he got wiped out here, he wondered how soon word would get to his brother Rick, somewhere down around Fort Fred Steele with Sam's former infantry company. Rick would feel sorry, no doubt, but he would not be surprised, for he had given his wild young brother up for lost when the latter threw in with Rocky Mountain Shorty.

Sam wondered how the Sioux had come to know just where the beaver pelts were hidden away. That cache had been cunningly dug and concealed. So far as Sam knew, nobody had even known that the party was adventuring into this part of the Big Horns. But somehow, the Sioux had found out. They had bided their time, then struck like wild hawks falling from the sky on crouching rabbits.

The buck on the yellow pony was near enough now. He could feel the smooth brown stock of the Henry against his cheek. The hammer was drawn to full cock and the pressure of finger on trigger felt comforting. He looked through the sights. The Sioux chief was a bold one, a broad lanky rider with a single eagle feather in his black hair. On his naked breast was painted a medicine sign in blood red that looked to Sam like a crude figure of a pitching pony.

Sam dug his knee deeper into the sod for a steadier stance. This move proved unwise. He had momentarily forgotten the arrow sticking in his flesh. He flinched as he fired and knew as he pulled off that he had not blown that painted medicine sign off the oncoming buck's breast as had been his intent.

He had dumped the rider off the yellow pony. The buck bunched up and rolled like a spitting wildcat into the cover of a clump of raspberry brush the moment he struck the ground. The yellow pony, pop-eyed with fear, rushed on past Sam toward the timber, dragging from its lower jaw the long rawhide thong of the war bridle.

Sam wanted to sing but he couldn't spare breath for it. He jumped up on his long legs. He was firing rapidly, barely flipping rifle stock to shoulder before he snapped the hammer. Indians hated point blank fire. They had shown the long hair they were not afraid to come out and fight. Maybe they'd go back in the brush now and try to starve Sam out.

He was counting on that. He sprayed the oncoming line of braves with his lead. He knocked over a pony at the far end of the line, and saw another whooping rider go spinning headlong into the sod. They had come in so near now that he could see the big round eyes of the ponies, and their flaring red nostrils. Smoke from the Henry circled up, but the haze could not hide the painted faced of the Sioux, their mouths wide open as they shrilled their defiance.

When he killed the pony, he broke the heart of the first rush. They veered off to both flanks, swinging low so that the bodies of their ponies barricaded them from this long hair's far reaching bullets. They dashed down to the stream and into the willow brush.

Never taking time for a breather, Sam turned and made a headlong run toward the looted beaver cache. The hole was a good six feet deep. When his moccasins touched the rim, he took a header into the cavity.

He crouched for a moment, panting like a hound, feeling the hammering of his heart against his ribs, feeling too the white hot burn of that confounded arrowhead. Knowing they'd try another rush if he didn't show himself in fighting position, he staggered up, and laid the hot barrel of the Henry on the edge of the pit.

He saw the pony he had killed, still kicking in its death agony not far down the grassy slope to Sam's right. Apparently the Sioux were in the willows also getting their breath, planning the next move against the long hair who sang so boldly.

Sam's first move was to reload his rifle, then check on the spare ammunition in his belt or the leather pouch he carried on his belt.

His hasty check showed that he possessed thirty rounds of soft-nosed .44 which would kill a heap of Sioux. He lined the shell up on the edge of the pit within easy reaching distance if he were forced to reload hurriedly. You never knew about Indians. They might try another headlong charge if he could work them up to it. His jeers had flushed them before. The sun was getting pretty hot and Sam's mouth began to feel like it was filled with cotton. He heard the clear soft chuckle of cool creek water rippling over stones, and licked his parched lips feeling the first gnawing pangs of battle thirst.

He became aware, as the fighting fog cleared from his brain, and the pain of his wound increased, that he was not the only person inside the looted beaver cache. The owner of the naked brown leg also occupied part of the pit. Sam felt the gentle pressure against the back of his legs. He could feel the skin crawling on the back of his neck as he turned around.

The naked brown body had been crammed head down into the pit. The face and head were hidden from Sam because a metal water bucket had been pushed down over the head. But Sam saw, from bodily contours, that this was not the Indian woman, not Tom Bear Mouth's sister, the Night Star. Quite likely this was her husband, the Buffalo Hump.

A touch of the flesh gave Sam's hand a clammy feeling. The Hump had been dead for several hours. Not far distant to the rear of the cache loomed the quaking asp patch in which had been built the log winter shack. Rank smoke still eddied from the grove. Sam's heart felt as cold now as the Hump's dead body. He was wondering about the fate of the Night Star. Indians were not often nice in their handling of female captives. Since they had discovered the cache and taken away a small fortune in pelts, Sam decided that first they had ambushed the Hump when he came down for water at dawn. Then they had tortured his wife into showing them the location of the cache.

For all Sam knew her naked dead body might be in the charred ruins of the shack. Or she might be a brutalized captive of the Sioux, bound and gagged down in the willows.

Sam turned a little sick thinking about the comely Night Star. There had been idle hours during the long winter in camp when Sam had envied the luck of Buffalo Hump. But he had early discovered that the Night Star was faithful to her husband. Shorty had discovered the same thing.

If Sam Sling hadn't reckoned himself as too cagey for Sioux and too smart to be run out of the mountains by soldiers, he wouldn't be here in this black hole this moment. Buffalo Hump and Night Star would still be alive, enjoying the fine June weather. Sam swore that if he came out of this with his hair on his head, he'd not set another beaver trap until he had killed or been killed by the murderers of the Indian man and woman.

If Tom Bear Mouth lived to discover the tragedy that had overtaken his sister and her mate, he'd blacken his face and hair with soot and ashes, and take to the vengeance trail. For Tom would reckon that the Sioux had dishonored his family. So long as the spirit of the scalped Buffalo Hump roamed the Happy Hunting Ground unavenged, Tom Bear Mouth's big medicine would continue powerless. He would be a pariah even among his own people.

The shaft of the arrow sticking out of Sam's hunting shirt bothered him. He seized it, and gave a mighty pull hoping he could dislodge the head. He felt his toes curl up and the icy sweat run down the insides of his legs. The arrow head wouldn't come out. It was there at least until Sam could find time to remove his shirt and operate with his skinning knife.

He took a deep breath when the sharp pain of his lacerated flesh had died down, gripping the shaft firmly with his left hand. Using his knife, he hacked off the shaft up to his body. Now he could swing around in his pit without jarring the wound each time the shaft touched the dirt walls.

He hated to take another look at the Buffalo Hump, for the brown body smeared with half dried blood kept reminding him that he had led this man to death. He wished that he could remove the Hump from the pit but the Sioux were giving him no time for that.

Sam had sung for the Sioux. Now they sang for him. He understood enough of the lingo to know they were taunting him. He had laughed and called them a pack of squaws. He had dared them to come out and fight like men. They had come out. But the long hair, the bold singer, had not stayed very long to fight. He had run and jumped into a hole like a prairie dog. The Sioux sang to Sam Sling that they had believed he could stand up and catch bullets in his hands, and that his medicine was very strong. But it looked as though the Sioux had been mistaken. He was a prairie dog, not a bold Big Medicine Singer. He had gone into his hole and wouldn't come out.

The combined pangs of the arrowhead wound and thirst put a wire edge on Sam's temper, which at no time was considered calm. Holed up with a murdered friend, he felt his hackles rise with ire. He brought the rifle stock to his shoulder (hot-livered, Shorty had said), to give them a lick or two. But he had been too long on the Great Plains and in the mountain country to lose his cool so easily. They were counting on that. A bullet saved now might mean the difference between life and death before this standoff ended.

He vowed that he wouldn't shoot recklessly nor expose himself unless he saw a fair chance to down a couple of Sioux. When the warriors understood they could not draw him from his hole with mockery, they fell silent. Sam knew they were planning new tactics. They might attempt another rush but he didn't think so. They had left a dead pony sprawled in the grass. And he had sent their chief crawling into that patch of berry brush and rocks over to his left. Sam wondered if the chief was still hiding there. He couldn't see any ripple of movement in the bushes to indicate that the man lived.

If he hadn't flinched from the sharp pain of that tarnal arrowhead, Sam felt certain he would have shot out the heart of the chief. His sights had covered that horse painted on the chief's bare breast. At that range, he would never have missed. He had knocked over running bull elk with a single shot at twice that range. He thought he might take time out to compose a new verse for the Sioux, calling on them not to act like squaws but to come out and get their chief.

But with the cold feeling of Hump's body against the back of his legs, poetic fancy didn't come easily to Sam's mind. The Sioux tried another trick on him. Far down the valley, a good two hundred yards away, three of the painted horsemen cantered out of the brush. The one who led waved a long feathered lance over his head. Something black, like a bundle of tarred rope, dangled from the tip of the lance.

The Sioux who were hiding in the brush taunted Sam, explaining to him that the black object on the lance was the scalp of the Buffalo Hump. The Hump, they pointed out, had been dishonored by being scalped. When the warrior who had killed him died, and went to the Happy Hunting Grounds, the Hump would be his slave for eternity.

But if Sam Sling could take the hair of the killer of the Hump, then the Hump would live on honorably in the Indian paradise. They were telling the truth to Sam. He knew enough about their beliefs to understand that. They were inviting him to kill the warrior who toted the lance, and avenge his scalped friend.

They succeeded in arousing Sam's anger. He studied the three horsemen closely. They were within range of the Henry but were unaware of the carrying power of Sam's gun. These Sioux were armed for the most part with old trade muskets, guns with worn out barrels from which they fired the lead slugs they had moulded. Some of the Sioux were picking up magazine rifles and fixed ammunition but finding it difficult since few white men would furnish them with modern fire arms.

The Indian rider who trailed the carrier of the scalp trotted nearer to Sam. He came out into a patch of sunlight which revealed that he was wearing a blue army blouse. Brass buttons flashed in the sun. With his keen eyes Sam could even make out white chevrons on the sleeves indicating the former owner of the blouse had been an infantry non-commissioned officer.

The leading Sioux singer in the willow patch now informed Sam that the coat had come from a walkaheap soldier down on the Platte River who had foolishly attempted to ride a pony. Walkaheaps were not men enough to ride horses so the Sioux had stampeded the pony and the soldier had been thrown off and lost his coat.

This song wound up with a brassy sound that amazed Sam. It was the bray of an army bugle. That had been Sam's first job when he was very young army kid. He had been windjammer with the infantry. So far as he knew, he had never known an Indian who could pucker up his expertly enough to blow a bugle. Either a white man had shown a Sioux buck how to sound a bugle, or a white renegade was with this war party. The fleeting thought came to Sam that this might also explain why the Sioux had been able to find the winter camp. It was just possible that Sam or his partner had dropped an unwise hint which had set some renegade on their trail into the Big Horns.

He had been willing enough to take his discharge and

get away from army red tape and regulations. But many men still served in the army who were his friends. Nor could Sam forget that his older brother also wore infantry chevrons. For the honor of his old regiment, he would risk one bullet on the wearer of the blue coast.

He switched the Henry barrel around to cover the horseman who had now come within a hundred yards. The light was good and the front sight stood aimed onto the blue and brass of the coat which covered the breast of the jeering buck.

This shot would also be one for the Buffalo Hump, Sam was thinking, as he began to take up trigger slack slowly. The buck's pony kept shifting as it advanced. Sam wanted a dead sure shot so he was waiting. As he pulled off he was suddenly deafened by another cannon-like roar from the patch of quakers.

He saw the buck in the blue blouse plunge head first off his horse as though he had run into a rock wall. Nor did this buck roll like a bobcat when he hit the bunch grass. He lay motionless there among the buttercups and the daisies with the June sun shining straight down on his blue walkaheap coat.

CHAPTER 3

That was the last shot fired for the day in the battle of the Beaver Meadow. Sam's mates had not deserted him. Working their way cautiously down through the timber, as they had earlier advised Sam to do, they had taken up position in the quaker grove to the rear of Sam's rifle pit. At the crucial moment, when a bullet would count the most, Rocky Mountain Shorty had gotten into the fight with old Susy, his heavy caliber buffalo gun.

The death of the buck who wore the blue coat of a soldier took the edge off the courage of the Sioux braves. While daylight lasted, they made no further attack, hiding in the willow brush. The two bucks who had ridden out with the man in the blue coat whipped their ponies around and fled into timber west of the creek.

The afternoon sun felt hot as fire to Sam. He told himself that he would have traded his right arm for a long drink of cold creek water. But there was no present way of getting a drink. His wound pained him. He knew that it required attention but he could not alone maneuver a knife to cut out the arrowhead. That must wait on Shorty and Tom Bear Mouth. They would not expose themselves just to save Sam a little suffering.

They had already risked their hair just by hanging around.

Sam had lost his slouch hat during the fight. He wrapped a dirty red bandanna around his head to keep the sun from cooking his brains, and to prevent the sweat from running down into his shooting eye.

All he heard from his friends, after Shorty had let go with Susy, was a command from the old mountaineer to stay in hole until dark came on.

"We'll try to get out then," said Shorty.

The long painful wait with a dead friend, in a narrow heated pit, gave Sam plenty of time for hard thought. A sense of guilt grew in him that he was to blame for this tragedy which had overtaken the expedition. If he hadn't discovered this spot of virgin trapping range, chances were that Buffalo Hump and his wife would be alive this minute over on the Wind River reservation with their Shoshone people.

It was a new feeling to Sam Sling. He had always pursued an independent course of life since he had become an orphan in boyhood and taken to selling newspapers on the streets of St. Louis. When Rick had persuaded him to enlist in the army after the close of the war, Sam had seen it as a chance for adventure. The skeletonized regiments were being moved to western outposts to curb Indians, and to guard the new transcontinental railroad being pushed toward the Pacific.

Sam had served his hitch honorably enough, but four years ago he had taken his discharge and thrown in his lot with Rocky Mountain Shorty. Army rules and red tape irked his youthful impulsiveness. He wished to be as free as the winds of the mountains. Rick, a professional soldier, had regretted Sam's scorn of service regulations but they had parted as friends.

Burning with thirst and the fever of his wound, looking grimly down the green slope to where the painted foe crouched, feeling against his legs the cold meat of a scalped friend, Sam wondered what Rick would say if he had happened along this moment with an army patrol.

Rick might blame him for getting friends into a pack of trouble, but Rick was always the cool reflective type, the sort of a man who kept most of his thoughts to himself. Rick had learned to control his tongue and temper in long years of war during which time he had risen from private to ranking duty sergeant of his company. He held the high esteem of his commanding officer. When Sam had quit the army, it was taken for granted that Rick Sling would be boosted to first sergeant when veteran Luke McNeal retired. That had been four years ago. Perhaps this moment Rick was taking it easy in the orderly room down at Fort Fred Steele, running Sam's former company.

Thinking of the old army turned Sam's thoughts to the bugle down in the brush. Since that first derisive blast, the Sioux had quit serenading him. He decided that quite likely the stunning punch of Susy, the buffalo gun, had convinced them that the walkaheap music and coat were not such mighty medicines.

The art of windjamming seemed to Sam to be confined to the pale-faces. Indians sang and blew on their little whistles fashioned from buffalo and bird bones. They pounded their rawhide drums when they danced for war or to honor the sun. But none were buglers. Puckering up and hardening the lips to draw musical strains from a bugle was painfully acquired through long hours of instruction.

With a frown, Sam recalled that he had received his first instructions from Corporal Bootle, ranking field musician of his battalion of infantry. It wasn't until

Sam had officially been raised from private to bugler, that he had discovered his instructor was envious of Rick Sling. It appeared that Bootle had considered himself ripe for promotion to sergeant but Rick had been given the post. This was before Sam enlisted.

Being in charge of the musicians, Bootle began taking out his anger against Sam Sling, the younger brother. Sam found himself being detailed to extra duty. This was when he first began blaming the army for regulations. Bootle was a non-commissioned officer, and a smooth one. Sam couldn't protest without being characterized as a sort of crybaby. It was army style for a man to work out his own troubles.

An infantry company was not mounted but had many pack animals on the rolls. Bootle saw to it that young Sam was often detailed as a helper to the stable sergeant. It was dirty work, cleaning up along picket lines, and in barns after horses and mules. Bootle, a fat arrogant type, seemed to enjoy dropping in as Sam labored with pitchfork and shovel, to inspect work, and often required the young soldier to do the job all over again. It was petty tyranny but it was not uncommon in the army. Sam bore it all silently.

But there came a day when he was alone with Bootle in the stable. This time, the fleshy corporal jeered at Sam, saying that he relied on his brother's rank to get away with poor work on a detail. Without a word, Sam knocked out Bootle's wind by hitting him in his paunch with the hickory handle of his pitchfork.

When Bootle staggered up, stuttering that he would have Sam tried before a general court-martial for attacking a superior officer, Sam grinned and knocked him down again.

Bootle proved too fat and short of wind to fight. He emerged from the stable with his eyes blackened and his mouth so swollen that he could not blow a bugle for a month. He preferred charges against Sam but since there had not been witnesses, he could not bring Sam to trial. Rick had questioned Sam about the fight but Sam had held his tongue. He had warned Rick to keep an eye on Bootle.

Sam couldn't know that the company commander had called on Rick for advice at the time when Bootle tried to prefer charges. Rick had pointed out the law that protected his brother. Captain Budhouse could not pass up the evidence of Bootle's black eyes. He therefore eased off the matter by confining Sam to barracks for a month, and giving him plenty of extra duty which was considered by old heads of the service to be the best method of taking the vinegar out of impulsive recruits.

But Bootle knew that Rick had defended Sam. His enmity against the older Sling had increased. He lived for the day when he could discover something that would tear down Rick Sling's hard-won reputation as a soldier and cause him to be dishonorably discharged or reduced in rank.

Some of Sam's soldier friends told Sam all about Bootle's underhanded work after he had taken his discharge. So when he took his discharge it had not been entirely his own personal grudge against the army. He loved his older brother as a son loves a father. He thought that Bootle should be exposed. But he knew that he dared not usurp Rick's right to protect himself. Rick was all man and soldier and lived by the code that he could protect himself at all times.

So Sam had thrown in with Rocky Mountain Shorty and trailed off to wander the Great Plains and the mountains, kill buffalo, trap beaver and wolves, serve now and then as a scout with an army expedition, or join a wagon train and drive a four-up of army mules. He had learned about Indians from Shorty, and had discovered many things about them the hard way as he was being instructed this hot day in the looted beaver cache.

The beaver meadow had yielded rich returns for the winter catch but a fortune in pelts, Sam told himself, was not worth a single hair of Buffalo Hump's scalp. He dared not reflect upon the fate of handsome Night Star. She might be dead and scalped or a poor dishonored captive in the hands of the Sioux raiders.

If Sam and his friends got out of these lonely mountains with hair on straight, they would receive no consolation or aid from the army. This entire country was barred against white civilians by federal regulations. The land had been lawfully turned over to the Sioux by treaty. The army had spread its forces along the reservation line to block eager white settlers from reaching Montana by way of the Bozeman Road through the Powder River country, or getting to the Black Hills mines by way of Hat Creek and the Cheyenne river.

Army patrols continually scouted the vast range, arresting and turning back trespassing settlers. Mountain men like old Shorty and Sam took some pleasure in scoffing at army regulations. They knew the mountains and the deserts like the backs of their own ponies. They risked their scalps, and ran their own chances for grubstakes in pelts.

But now the Sioux war party had the bulk of the winter's work, and had dishonored Tom Bear Mouth by scalping his brother-in-law. Bear Mouth would not set another beaver trap until he had restored his lost honor by avenging himself for the Hump's death and whatever fate had befallen his sister.

Sam knew by the code of the mountain men that he

had to follow Tom's lead. There would be no more quick stakes when they blew into Canada Pete or some other wild west fence. They would kill or be killed by the Sioux before they resumed their free and easy life in the west.

The Sioux made no move to bring in the body of the warrior who wore the blue coat. Nor did they attempt a rescue of the wounded brave who had ridden the yellow pony. The long hours passed until darkness fell. In the early darkness, Sam crept from his hole and snaked back into the quakers where Shorty and Tom were waiting.

Knowing the Indians feared roving around at night, having a superstitious belief that spirits of the dead then walked, Sam and his mates headed immediately for the high country where they had left the four pack horses. There was nothing to stay for. The cabin had been burned down. There was no trace of the Night Star. They dared not even take a chance by burying Buffalo Hump.

Tom Bear Mouth had smeared his hair and face with soot and ashes from the charred ruins of the cabin. This indicated his grief over Buffalo Hump and Night Star, and his vow not to resume a normal life until he had attained vengeance or been killed trying for it.

Sam spoke briefly of the guilt he felt for getting his friends into such a pickle. But Shorty and Tom had no blame. Tom was as silent now as an owl in the daytime. They had taken their chances when they followed him. It was not part of the mountain code to whine about hard luck. Mountain men, when disaster overtook them, loaded up and went gunning for those they blamed.

"Quit fightin' your head, bub," Shorty advised. "Put your mind to gittin' away from here and into hidin' by daybreak. Soon as it's first light, them war whoops will be hot and heavy on our tracks."

They had lost all their supplies except for the spare ammunition in their packs, the clothing on their backs, and the few pelts they had taken during the ill-timed trapping. They required these pelts to trade with Canada Pete for more ammunition and grub before they went after the Sioux killers.

Pete's trading post was located a mile west of Cantonment Sparks, an army outpost on the Oregon Trail along the North Platte. Sam and Shorty had picked up some beaver traps from Pete, the fall before, when they prepared for the trip into the Big Horns. They forsook Sam's pet horse, Baldy, not daring to scout around in the darkness for the animal. With Shorty and Tom leading their saddle horses, and Sam following along, shirt cinched to strap up his wound, they put in some rough hours climbing up through thick timber, and across old fire-burns where felled timber littered the earth. Toward daybreak, they found the pack horses. They paused only to eat a breakfast of jerked venison, washed down with water from a spring.

They crossed over the divide through a rocky snow-studded pass covered with slick rocks. They knew that they were now on the east slope of the Big Horns. All these small streams, fed by snowbanks and icy lakes, cut down through steep canyons, heading on an eastward course toward Powder River which lay many miles beyond the mountains. Since the Sioux were horsemen and hated foot work, the three trappers worked their way down the canyon afoot, choosing the roughest path over rocks, at times walking through icy snow water to hide tracks. They worked their stumbling pack horses over steep pitches and Sam apologized for his awkwardness. His left side had stiffened up. He could not perform an equal share of the hard work with his usual deftness.

"Come daylight," Shorty panted once when they were resting after working the string of horses down a neck-breaking fall of rock, "we'll look at that ar'er head. Right now, can't light a fire to work a knife. Chances are Injuns ain't out none in the dark but we jest can't take chances."

Dawn found them hidden out below steep canyon walls that rose for a thousand feet toward the blue sky. The roar of the stream sounded in their ears. Granite boulders as large as houses studded the banks of the stream. They huddled the pack stock and two saddle horses into the shadow of the rocks where signs indicated wild animals had found shelter.

Bear Mouth, huddling in a ragged blanket, sat on guard while Shorty took his knife, rubbed his thumb along it to test its edge, and operated on Sam. With barbed fangs at the base, the arrow head could not be drawn out the way it had entered. It was like a fish hook. Rather than waste time working it through Sam's flesh, Shorty made a couple of quick slashes that Sam felt clear to his toes. He handed the bloody head to Sam. He was grinning.

"Part of the shaft on it. Little paint marks show the buck what owned it. Some of it might tell you who he was."

"He had a bucking horse painted on his chest," grunted Sam. He was glad he could find something to talk about for Shorty's cutting had revived all the agony of his wound. "I think he was the chief. Figure I hit him but don't know how bad. But I'll put this thing in my pouch. Might help Tom to run down one of the bunch that kilt Hump."

CHAPTER 4

They wearied of the risky work of getting the string of horses down the canyon, when darkness fell. When the canyon broadened out toward dawn, they decided it was now safe to mount up without risking a broken neck or leg. Tom Bear Mouth, silent because of his grief, spoke briefly against it, saying that if light overtook them far out in open country, distant from possible fighting cover, Sioux scouts might sight them. But the two white men had grown impatient. Sam's wound was pushing his temper. Shorty was running short of tobacco. They knew they were at least sixty miles from Pete's post by the shortest route. They took to the horses at first opportunity.

Shifting some of the packs, Sam mounted up on a barrel-headed roan pack cayuse. The animal was hard-mouthed, rough-gaited, far different than Baldy. That increased Sam's ire.

Shorty advised him to forget his troubles and invent a new verse for his song. "Time to sing, Bub," he said, "is when you got lots of troubles. That is unless you're right near some place what you can likker up and j'ine female company."

When Shorty blew in his fur profits, his sprees were loud and lasted long. He was host to all men and women who would drink with him.

"Been a long time," he said wistfully, "since I had a real good time. Last time was down around Fort Steele. That's when I first met you, Bub. You and a young soldier was in trouble with some tinhorn gamblers."

Sam recalled that night. His friend, Spike Dillon, had seized a gambler's wrist after losing a month's pay at cards, and shaken an ace from the dealer's cuff. Another house man had knocked out Spike with a pistol stock. Sam had waded into the fight with both fists. He was outmatched. It was then that old Shorty, half-drunk but willing, knocked out the light, giving Sam a chance to pack his senseless bunky from the dive.

"Chicago Jack's place," mused Sam. "Bootle was corporal of the guard that night. When me and Spike got back to the post, Bootle threw us both in the mill. Cap. Budhouse—us boys had nicknamed him Bughouse—gave us both thirty days on kitchen police and the honey duty around the fort."

"Jack's a hot sport," said Shorty. "He wouldn't mind turnin' a crooked card to win a soldier's pay. Or any other man's money. But he wasn't in the joint that night. Looked to me like your bunky was framed on to get you rookies into plenty trouble. You was both packin' guns. You started to pull a pistol when I went for the lantern. If you's kilt that tinhorn, the army would likely have hung you higher'n a kite."

"But they had knocked out Spike."

"None of them tinhorns woulda been your witnesses if you'd kilt one of 'em savin' Spike. Anyways, you told me later the joint was plumb off bounds to soldiers. That's why your captain flang you in the guard-house, and made you sweat it out on a garbage wagon."

Sam began thinking about his army bunkies, wondering what had happened to Spike and another close friend with whom he had spreed around. That was Jimmy Kerry. They had enlisted the same day and taken recruit drill together in Jefferson Barracks in Missouri before being assigned to the old regiment in Wyoming Territory. Well, a man had enjoyed some fun now and then in the old army, despite the red tape, and met a few good-hearted characters. He felt glad Shorty had avenged some poor soldier by putting a buffalo gun slug through the boaster who wore a doughboy's coat.

It was a strange thing about army service, he mused, as his awkward pack horse trailed after old Shorty's mount down a game trail through creek brush. Longer a man was away from the monotony of barracks and hard tack and fat bacon, more he recalled the good friends he had known, and the times he had enjoyed with them, spending the few dollars they had drawn in hard earned pay.

But he also reflected that if he encountered army friends now, men like gay Spike Dillon and Jimmy Kerry, even his brother, Rick, they'd be forced to arrest him, run him out of Sioux treaty land. They'd do it in an impersonal way. They wouldn't hold a grudge because he had risked his life to break an army law and win a rich stake in beaver. Maybe, after he got south of the line, they'd even join him in a drink.

Shorty poulticed Sam's wound with a chaw of fresh tobacco and fluff from a beaver pelt, then strapped it up tightly with the tail of Sam's undershirt so Sam could travel easier. Sam tried not to flinch but once or twice he ground out a curse.

"Try some of your singin'," Shorty advised. "Cracklin', Bub. What's a little old ar'er head amount. Blackfeet put one smack dab in old Jim Bridger's back plumb over the kidney's. Jim's carried it for y'ars and y'ars. But he's chipper this minute as a squirrel and got married three times since and raised a couple of families. Take a chaw terbaccer, Bub. Rest easy. Our troubles are jest startin'."

When they broke from the mountains into open plains country east of the range, the Sioux would be given a chance to overtake them, maybe make a kill if they caught the three trappers in some position where they couldn't make a good standoff.

Tom Bear Mouth, vigilant in the mouth of the rock overhang that hid the horses, motioned with his soot smeared head, then pointed silently with his chin to the rim of the high canyon wall above them. Sam and Shorty, grasping their rifles, lay without speaking, eyes on that granite rim which appeared so near the blue sky of Wyoming.

They counted ten Indians pass along the top of the wall riding in single file. The sun light illuminated their painted bodies, the colors of their horses, even the eagle feathers they wore in their hair. Sam drew in his breath sharply when he noted that one warrior wore a blue army coat, that another was bestriding a yellow pony. But what most aroused his anger was that one of the Indians was leading his buckskin buffalo horse, Baldy.

"Now," growled Shorty, when the Sioux had disappeared. "They're ahead of us. From now on, we'll be dodgin' either Injuns or soldiers until we can hide out in Pete's place on the Platte."

That turned his thoughts again to the bugle he had heard. He couldn't believe that one of his friends had thrown in with the Sioux. Of course plenty of soldiers could blow a bugle after a fashion. There were long monotonous hours in barracks at these lonely western outposts like Cantonment Sparks. Soldiers tried every sort of fancy that could make them forget hard service and monotony. Some learned to play a few garrison calls although they did not rate as buglers. It might be that some soldier, in jest, had taught an Indian how to blow a bugle.

But it was a remote possibility. Doughboys didn't jest around with Sioux bucks. The Sioux had taken too many doughboy scalps in the fights up around Fort Phil Kearny. They had also lost plenty good warriors to the doughboys in that wagon-box fight. Hostile Indians and soldiers wasted no love on one another. It would be unusual to teach a Sioux how to play a bugle.

Where had the Sioux found the bugle? Perhaps in the same fight in which they had taken the blue blouse. There were white renegades in this land who often threw in with hostiles for purposes of their own. The trade in repeating rifles was brisk since the hostiles had discovered the extra speed and utility of magazines and fixed ammunition. It was rumored that a trader could sell a magazine rifle for a small fortune in beaver, buffalo hides, or ponies. However, even though the Indians used these guns mainly to kill off soldiers and settlers, few mountain men would join in such trade. There were some things that even these hardened mountaineers would not do to win a quick stake. They didn't particularly care how many soldiers were killed, but they would have no part in speeding up Indian styles of execution.

If some white renegade had persuaded the Sioux that the blue coat and bugle were strong war medicine, enough to tempt a war party into the Big Horns, then the renegade had gone against his own kind for the fortune hidden in the cache. Sam frowned. The fate of the Night Star also entered into the murder picture. She was a handsome woman. She was true to her husband. But women were scarce along the Platte. Some white renegade might have planned the raid to win the Night Star for himself.

Because of their impatience to reach safety along the Platte, they were caught by full daylight far out from the mountains. They were traversing a rough country of red shale hills spotted with twisted cedars. There was not much cover. Far to the east, they could see the Black Hills as a hazy line along the eastern horizon. To their south lay the upper prong of the North Platte where it made the big bend after the junction with Sweetwater. They had tied the three pack horses nose to tail in single file. Shorty brought up the rear, whipping on the pack stock with the braided end of a lash rope. Tom Bear Mouth rode in the lead, ever on the alert, hooded black eyes seeking Sioux signs.

The string of men and horses dropped through one narrow gap in a red rock wall. They came out into a shallow sagebrush valley, crossing it toward a steep rocky ridge running from north to south, with the southern end dominated by a flat-topped butte.

Without a word, Tom Bear Mouth set his course toward the butte, and began to lash his tired pony down both sides with his quirt. Shorty was giving all get out to the galloping pack stock. One pony lost a bale of beaver where canyon rocks had cut a lash rope. They did not pause to recover the pelts.

The sun was slanting down. It was now a murderous revealing glare. They were caught in a poor spot for a standoff on broken tired horses. They didn't wish to desert their packs. They hoped that they could climb up on the butte and barricade in the rocks before Sioux horsemen overtook them. As Shorty yelled above the thunder of hoofs on the hardpan, he could smell Sioux as thick on the air as a buffalo dead three weeks.

With the wind blowing from the north, Sam stuck to that flank so that he would not be blinded by dust kicked up by the galloping horses. Every jump of his rough riding pony sent a shaft of pain through his frame but he knew that he must bear the pain and ride for his life.

He couldn't spot a Sioux sign in all the vast land which appeared so warm and peaceful under the June sun. But his friends were wise to Indian ways through years of risky experience. They seemed to possess a sixth sense so far as hostiles were concerned.

Tom Bear Mouth, selecting the top of the butte as a natural fort, had headed up a natural incline while the others followed. In this rolling country where mountains gave way to the Great Plains, the sagebrush grew high and rough. Sam felt it brush his moccasins as his pony galloped ahead. Prairie dogs were chattering at their burrows throughout the warm valley. He hoped that his clumsy bare-footed horse wouldn't stumble and fall over on of these dog holes.

Sam was not certain just where to keep an eye peeled for the Sioux attack. All he knew for certain was that the war party had ridden ahead of the trappers as the latter hid in the mountain canyon. He did know how crafty the Sioux were, highly skilled in war tactics, acclaimed by military men as the finest natural cavalry that the world had seen. They might hit from either flank, from the front, or come dashing in from the rear.

A favorite war method of red raiders was to scatter a party—as Sam's outfit was now strung out—then dash in and cut off the leader or the man who brought up the rear. Or if a man ventured too far out on the flank they would cut in between him and the main party. Where the ground was hard and not dangerous for horses, the Sioux excelled in war.

The sagebrush grew thick down below the rocky ridge but sagebrush was not thick enough to turn aside war arrows or slugs fired from old muskets. Nor would it break up a rush of war ponies.

Tom Bear Mouth had selected the top of the butte as the nearest life saving cover, and was now riding his pony down to a whisper to reach that position.

These horses were tired and hungry from the long journey down from the high mountain country. They had found short grazing during the various hideout camps as they could not be hobbled and turned out to hunt grass. All these horses were of the Indian breed. Not one had tasted oats or corn in his life. For the past few weeks they had grown pot-bellied and soft on the lush green grass of spring-time mountain meadows.

The frenzied speed to which they were now forced, began to tell on the ponies. Sweat stood on their ribs and flanks like soap lather. Sam felt the faltering beneath him of his hard-running mount. If the pony gave up, Sam knew he would be an easy target for the Sioux arrows.

Hanging to the bitter dust of the rear, Shorty gave his full attention to the pack horses. He trusted in his comrades to keep an eye open for Indians. Shorty had lost one bale of beaver pelts on this run. He was a grim old realist. He would not give further tribute to the Sioux without a fight.

The sides of the butte were steep. Sam understood well enough that the stern test would come when the horse must be forced to climb its peak. He could see that it was not inaccessible. It was threaded with the narrow slanting trails worn through the grass during long centuries by pasturing herds of buffalo and other wild game. These angling trails would offer access to the top of the butte.

But wild game climbed or descended steep trails at a leisurely pace unless pursued by natural enemies. If the Sioux struck before Tom Bear Mouth rode out on the butte mesa, the horses would be forced to exert all the strength and heart they possessed to climb the steep slope.

A mountain man seldom jumped blindly into a fight with Indians. He lived to green old age, if he was lucky, by planning ahead. The two white men, yielding to their inherited Anglo-Saxon impatience, had forced themselves into a trap which might close at any moment. Sam Sling, through impulsiveness, had shown plenty of white bravery which would have amounted to nothing at all if Shorty and Tom hadn't risked their own hair to extricate him from the beaver cache.

Sam was well aware of all this as his horse bore him through the brush. He had determined that he owed a large debt to his two friends, even to the scalped Hump and the missing Night Star. He planned his further course of action with that in mind. He was young, and to him the sweet June breeze, and the sun pouring down on this wild free western world were precious. Life meant far more to young Sam Sling than to old Shorty or to grieving Tom Bear Mouth. Age had, as the poet put it, withered Shorty's infinite variety. Since the loss of his honor, life to Tom had become only an existence, bitter as the ashes smeared on his braided scalp locks.

The infantry didn't train its soldiers as horsemen. But Sam had picked up all the tricks of a rider in the four years he had ridden the mountain country with Shorty. He figured he was jockey enough to whip his horse to a white lather and outride Tom to the top of the butte.

Shorty would hang to the bales of pelts while he could. The loss of his entire outfit to the hated Sioux, even if he saved his own hair, would be as great a disgrace to the mountain man as the murder of Buffalo Hump had been to Tom Bear Mouth.

The unshod hoofs boomed on the hard earth. The wolfish yelp of a Sioux scout, even near at hand, could not have been heard by the three gallopers. Sam hung his chin on his shoulder for a look over the back trail. But he had long since decided that the Sioux would not be coming from that direction. More likely they would be hidden on some flank, waiting for the trappers to come to them.

Shorty's gun, old Susy, carried a powerful kick. But Susy was a single-shot rifle. If Shorty fell back to fight a rearguard action, he would get in one lick and kill one warrior before they rode him down.

Sam knew that Shorty was stubborn. He would not easily give up his post because of honor. He legs were somewhat stiff with age. His heart and lungs had lost the vitality of youth. Shorty would require all his power—like one of the pack-horses—to climb to the top of the butte.

Before the Sioux launched the flank attack, Sam turned his pony toward Shorty and the string of galloping pack ponies. Then the warriors of the Sioux came tearing down at an angle from the crest of the long bar ridge which was dominated by the butte. They had hidden up there, waiting for the critical moment to arrive, when they could most easily cut the white men away from cover, catch them strung out and off balance, and crush them in a wild charge.

The Sioux tore in from Sam's flank as Tom struck the first rocky pitch at the butte's base. The rolling dust hid the line of attack from Shorty's view except for momentary glimpses in the eddying haze. Shorty was yelling madly, wearing out his rope on the last pack horse in the string.

With crafty eye, Tom had selected the slanting trail that promised the easiest grade for running horses to the top of the butte. It would be a cruel climb of at least a hundred paces, but there was a chance of getting to cover if the Sioux could be brushed off in their first rush.

Riding in, Sam bent to the side and whipped up Shorty's mount. The mountain man, feeling his steed's sudden frightened gain in speed, swung in his saddle with a yell. He was staring into Sam's grim face. Shorty made a movement as though to halt his horse. But Sam quirted the old man's horse vigorously down the hind legs. Shorty, without time to pull back on bridle reins, was carried headlong across a narrow dry wash filled with brush and rocks in the wake of the clattering pack string.

The line of horses were crowding up the trail close on the heels of Tom Bear Mouth. Whatever had been Shorty's plan for the final round of this flight, Sam had driven him to where he could not pause until he had reached cover.

While Tom and Shorty and the laden horses puffed and sweltered their way up the side of the butte, dislodging rocks that crashed down through the brush and sparse growth of cedar, Sam opened his rearguard action.

He jumped his pony into the clear, away from the billowing dust that was bitter with alkali. He swept across the narrow wash at an angle and chose a broken pile of rocks that would temporarily serve as a rude barricade. As his pony floundered past the rocks, Sam swung to the ground. He lit almost on the run, flung his body in back of his shelter, and rammed the Henry stock to his shoulder.

Only by split seconds had Tom Bear Mouth won the wild race for the foot of the butte. The Sioux had expected that they could ride in and pick off men and horses straggling up the steep hill. They had not expected that one pale-face would dismount and protect the other two.

CHAPTER 5

The Sioux came in on the jump, flattened out along the backs of their hard running little ponies. Expecting to cut off the three trappers, one by one, as they sought to climb the peak, the warriors were confused now by Sam's sudden change of plan. It was one thing to cut a man off a climbing horse, another to ride a pony straight up to the smoking black muzzle of a magazine rifle.

The Sioux didn't like it. They came fanning across the dry wash in a rolling haze of dust while Singin' Sam was cutting the haze with a string of bullets. Above the barking roll of his Henry, he heard the howls of the red riders, the scuffling hoofs of the wiry war ponies as the shaggy beasts slid down the steep slide of the wash then scrambled up the slope commanded by Sam.

Sam killed the first warrior who rode to his pile of rocks. He shot him through the middle, just above his navel, and the Sioux took a kicking headlong dive into the gravel of the wash.

"Wagh!" Sam roared, counting coup. "Wagh! The Sioux are squaws!"

One dead man proved enough for the moment. The raiders swerved away from the long hair's deadly gun that killed at a mile. Their war arrows rattled harmlessly off Sam's rocky barricade. They turned southward, riding so that they hung low from their ponies on the side away from Sam. He held his lead. He wasn't in this tight spot to shoot down horses.

Nor did he intend to hang around this patch of rocky cover while Sioux scouts, dismounting, slipped back to take him from the rear. He jumped up and began to climb the hill at an angle, quartering toward the south so that he could keep an eye on the Indians. In this rolling land, they could hide out almost instantly like rattlesnakes.

He was halfway up the hill and going at a dog trot around its face when he heard the shout of Rocky Mountain Shorty from the crest.

"Come on up! We got a hide-out! Everything fine 'ceptin' one pony with an ar'head in its rump!"

But Sam yelled in answer that he aimed to scout out the Sioux hiding placed before he rejoined. Shorty angrily disagreed, shouting in his high-pitched squawky voice. "No more of this white brave stuff! Hell! Up here we can stand off the hull Sioux nation!"

Sam persisted stubbornly in his scouting plan. He wished to spot the chief who rode the yellow pony if the man was still alive. Last time he had seen him go crawling for cover up in the beaver meadow. There was also the mystery of the bugle. And what about the Night Star? It was possible the woman was nearby, held captive by this war party.

Sam was not sure that the Sioux he had just fought were the men he had faced up in the mountains. The encounter on the bank of the dry wash had been too brief, too hazed up with dust and powder smoke to give a man time for any sort of identification. About all he knew was that the chief had a bucking horse painted on his breast, and that the hostiles possessed the blue blouse of a soldier, now decorated with a bullet hole.

The sun blazed down on Sam's sweaty back, for buckskin was hot down here in June in the foothills. He meditated on tearing off the dirty clinging hunting shirt but his bare skin would draw clouds of buffalo gnats and that would irritate a man far more than the stiffness of his wounded side.

He came around the southern end of the long ride, jogging on a narrow ledge above a shiny sheer wall of hot red rock. From this headland, perhaps fifty feet below the top mesa where Shorty and Tom were holed up, Sam took in a big scope of country.

To the east of the peak a long shallow valley ran north to south, then on across it, a quarter mile. Another rocky divide reared its saw-toothed hump further on. The valley was rough with rocks and prairie-dog holes hidden by stands of gray sagebrush.

The heat, and the bitter smoke of burnt powder had built up a powerful thirst in Sam's throat. The valley looked as dry as the Red Desert. He had quit his pony and the animal had stampeded carrying away his water bottle. Shorty and Tom had enough water up on the peak to see them through the day but Sam figured he was in for a dry session so long as the Sioux hid out around the foot of his ridge.

Some of them were smart enough to figure out Sam's gun range for he saw three of the painted horsemen to the west of his position. They were not within killing distance. But they were near enough so that he made out the flash of a blue coat in the sun on the warrior who topped off the yellow pony. One of the three was heavily blanketed. The thought came to Sam that this might be the missing Night Star, a captive held here to witness the wiping out of the two whites and her brother.

The wearer of the blue coat was apparently a chief for he carried a long lance with eagle feathers dangling from its tip. With this, he was signalling to his men. The main body of warriors had taken to cover. They had hidden their ponies in some coulee concealed from Sam. They might be under the observation of Shorty and Tom. Wherever they were, Sam knew they were busy as ants planning the most expeditious way of taking three scalps.

Alone here on this ledge, well aware that crafty Sioux might come boiling out from some concealed trail up the side of the slope, Sam felt no particular fear. If a man took time out to be afraid, he generally wound up with a bloody bald head. Best way to outwit the Sioux was to keep busy. Sam was as busy now as a thin dog with a bad case of fleas. He squirmed around the nose of the ledge and dropped off the point, falling ten feet straight down into springy sagebrush. For one instant he had been under the eyes of the chief who rode the yellow horse.

The moment he hit his sagebrush mattress, Sam balled up his arms and legs and forced his way through spiky branches to the damp ground. Beneath the cover of the sage was a green world concealed from the killing rays of the western sun. Here the grass grew green and tender. The earth was damp. All around Sam were the dainty trails of the tiny field mice and the chipmunks. Prairie-dogs, those loud chatterers, never built their homes in the sagebrush.

When he had crawled ten feet from where he had landed, Sam chose a patch of inky shadow. He snaked into it, and hid there, listening to every tiny sound that reached his ears.

But here within the great gray sagebrush jungle was a cavern of silence, that peculiar silence of the Great Plains which seems to ring like a distant silvery bell in a man's ears. Sam could not hear the rustle of the spring breeze in the leafy tops of the tall gray bushes. Hours seemed to pass, although he lay motionless and listening only a short time. Where a man could not see ahead for more than a few feet, his life depended upon his ears.

By dropping into the sagebrush, Sam had planned first to escape observation by the Sioux, then scout out the eastern face of the peak. Some trail, unknown to Tom and Shorty, might give the enemy opportunity to creep up and take them by surprise. Once Sam had satisfied himself that no painted warrior was nearby, he began a crawling course to the left, working his way slowly around the base of the butte. The ground rose gently. The brush began to thin out. Sam began encountering large rocks that had rolled down the slope of the peak.

One rock which Sam judged was the size of a small cabin barred his way. Thick brush grew all around it. Rather than snake around it, Sam began climbing over the rock. It felt hot as an oven, exposed to the merciless beat of the sun. Sam flattened out for an instant, flinching as his sore ribs touched hard rock. The sweat began seeping down into his narrowed eyes from his hair. He had taken off his red bandanna when he entered the brush, fearing the color would attract the keen eyes of hostile scouts.

After he had blinked the salt sting from his eyes, he cautiously raised his head for another look around. He discovered that he was high enough to scout out the long valley east of the peak.

What he saw a half mile northward up the valley amazed Sam. Perhaps it also accounted for the silence of the Sioux and explained why they had not more hotly pursued him. A dusty wagon train was rumbling slowly along the valley. The vehicles would pass Sam's front if he remained long enough on his hot rock.

He counted seven wagons in the string, all drawn by mule teams. A quarter mile ahead of the train, proceeding at a brisk pace toward him, Sam saw a light army ambulance drawn by a team of mules. He decided that the light vehicle had gone ahead to escape the stifling dust raised by the wheels of the train and the hoofs of trudging mules.

Sam knew these light, canvas-covered ambulances were as often used by the army for hauling sound men through the fenceless west as for the sick and wounded. A team of mules could pull an ambulance at a brisk pace. On hot days, the canvas sides could be rolled up to admit the breeze, or in wintry weather, tightly buttoned down to bar out the snow and cold.

Horsemen flanked the main train, holding their mounts to the slow pace set by the work teams.

Sam squinted his sun-dazzled eyes and growled under his breath. Some of those riders were not civilians. He could make out the heavy blue shirts and pants with which the army clothed its soldiers even in baking summer weather.

Where the three trappers had hoped to shake off the Sioux and strike for the Platte with the few pelts they had saved, the army barred the trail. If Sam and his friends were arrested on this Indian land, undoubtedly they would be relieved of their furs. The only hope of escape for the trappers was to hide on the butte, wait for the train to vanish, then take chances with the Sioux on getting to the Platte.

Sam knew that even with a scalping knife point in the small of his back, old Shorty would not have called on the army for rescue. His friends, high up on the peak, had undoubtedly spotted the rolling dust of the train long before he squirmed up on his rock. Since he was not under immediate threat Sam decided to crouch here and endure the heat and keep his vigilance.

It was odd, he thought, that this wagon train had come so far north into Sioux territory. He decided that the surrounding troopers indicated that some foolheaded party of settlers had made a break for the north, been overtaken and put under arrest by an army patrol, and forced to swing around for the long roll back to the Platte.

The thought did not bother Sam since he had little more time for wagon trains than for soldiers. These noisy emigrants frightened or wasted the game. They carelessly set fire to prairie grass, burning off good winter feed for the buffalo and antelope. They quite often got into a row with Indians that sent angry warriors blazing across the frontier eager for any white scalp they encountered. Most of the time a mountain man knew which Indians he could trust, but greenhorn settlers spiked the game for many a mountaineer and sent him to an untimely grave.

So Sam lay at ease, closely watching the approaching train. From the top of the ridge across the valley, he caught a flash of light from the corner of his eye. Instantly he was all attention. He set his eyes on the ridge and waited. The flash of light came again. He knew then that Sioux were over there, hidden on the ridge, using small hand mirrors to flash signals to braves hidden out near Sam.

Since he was sure they had not yet cut his trail, he decided the Sioux had scouted the train for hours, and with savage craft, had laid a trap for it. Seven wagons would be difficult to capture. But that ambulance, so far in the lead, would be easily cut off. The soldiers, Sam thought, were fools not to call it back once they had seen the Indian mirror signals. He waited for some sign that would indicate the men with the train had spotted the savage's signals.

But the seven wagons, each drawn by four mules, came on at a leisurely pace. The ambulance, drawing farther ahead, was now not too far to Sam's front. The wagoneers and guards had either not picked up the signals or, in ignorance, had disregarded these indications of danger.

Sam knew that if he flipped up the Henry and let go with a string of shots, he would spread such an alarm that he'd break up any Indian trap. He could fire off his Colt hand gun, warning the troopers of the enemies in sight. But once he raised smoke and noise, he stood good chances of losing his hair to some nearby Sioux, or—if he escaped with his life—being put under arrest by the army. He might draw Tom and Shorty into the fight, cause them to lose their pelts, and break up any immediate plan of running down the killers of the Hump.

It was not easy for Sam to decide to let the soldiers and the train roll into the Indian trap, or see the careless ambulance get cut off. After all, he had worn army blue and some of these indifferent guards might be men he had served with. It was not beyond the realm of possiblity that his brother, or his friends, Spike Dillon and Jimmy Kerry, were with the wagon train.

His old regiment was still stationed in Wyoming territory. Companies had been shifted north to the treaty line since pressure had ended along the transcontinental railroad line. It was not easy to crouch here in the sun on a bare rock and unfeelingly watch a train of white soldiers and civilians rumble into the clutches of the Sioux.

But he believed that he owed a deep debt to Tom Bear Mouth and old Shorty. They would not approve of any move by Sam which might break up their plans for revenge. They had not blamed him for luring them into the Big Horns but it would be against the mountain code to make any rash move that would throw them into the power of the army.

Sam began to wonder just what form the Sioux trap would take. Whopping Indians might dash from that ridge across the valley on their ponies. The wagon train would halt hastily and circle around into a corral for fighting. While that move was being made, while wagoneers and guards were vastly confused and excited, another force of Indians could dash in and out between the ambulance and the main train. The mule team would be stampeded into a crazed runaway. The ambulance would be upset by some rock striking wildly spinning wheels. Triumphant Sioux would canter off with the dripping scalps of whoever happened to be inside the ambulance, and whatever loot could be discovered in the vehicle.

Not that the Sioux cared much for stuff that pony soldiers valued. They would dare a company of infantry to get a gun but they'd dump out valuable white flour just to get the sacks. Indian squaws fashioned many glamorous garments from flour sacks.

The ambulance was not far from Sam. The mules were trotting along but he saw that they were tossing their long-eared heads nervously. Now and then he heard the snap of the driver's whip and the loud curses with which the man sought to quiet his team.

Mules quite often became nervous when around wild Indians. Somehow, Sam knew, they held the same distaste for the red men that their white masters did. The Indians, for their part, disliked mules. If they caught them, they killed them and roasted the flesh over their fires for a big feast. They seldom attempted to ride or pack the long ears so favored by the pony soldiers for carrying food and ammunition.

Sam became so interested watching the approaching mule team and waiting for flickers of light from the opposite ridge that he inched to the edge of his rock. He had sat there for several moments when he discovered that unwittingly, he had ventured into a portion of the Indian trap.

Directly beneath the overhang of his rock, a naked warrior crouched. The man was flat on his belly. He was so intent on watching the approaching train that he had not heard or seen the white man above him on the rock. Nor would Sam have found the Sioux if he had not been drawn to the rock's edge by his interest in what was about to happen.

The rock was hot enough to fry an egg but Sam froze. His body turned cold as ice for an instant. His first blinding thought was that the clever Sioux had forced him to reveal his position. Warriors might be crouching all around in the brush, grinning balefully as they drew their skinning knives and made ready to jump this ballad singer who had scorned them as squaws.

Then Sam relaxed. He was undiscovered for the moment. The warrior, crouching in the shade of the rock, gave no indication that he knew Sam was poised above him.

Sam took his sweaty grip off the Henry. The rifle would be clumsy in a hand to hand fight if one broke out. Rather, he would rely on the knife and Colt gun. He decided that he would drop off the top of the rock, land astride the Indian, and bury his knife between the brave's shoulder blades.

Then he decided against that style of attack. He must make a silent kill if he hoped to get out of this one alive. A knife in the back seldom resulted in silent loss of life. He had seen a man jump up and run a dozen yards with a knife sticking from his back. If he reached higher and got to the Indian's throat, the man would thrash around in the brush like a buffalo bull bogged in the mud while the blood gushed from his severed throat. But most of the time, Sam knew, if a man was hit hard in the right spot on the head, he sprawled out in instant paralysis of mind and muscle. He could slide off his rock easily enough. But he had to push the Indian and strike him an unerring blow before the warrior had time to yell an alarm.

Sam was just pulling up his legs and nerving himself for a drop from the rock when the Indian horsemen struck from across the valley. A dozen wild riders spurted down from the rocks and cedars of the opposite ridge. They sounded like a pack of hungry wolves as they drove straight toward the train.

Dust rose like smoke, and Sam heard the high shouts of wagoneers, and the crackle of gunfire as the seven wagons rumbled around to form a corral.

Obscured by the golden haze, Sioux riders split off and made for the ambulance. Their yells alarmed the mules. The team, straightening out in the traces, stampeded off to the side, galloping toward the sagebrush covered hill where Sam crouched above the Indian. This then was the Sioux plan. These hidden warriors would rush in on foot to stab and kill once their mounted mates had headed the mule team into the sagebrush. Before help could come from the train, the ambulance driver and any passengers in the vehicle would be scalped and dead.

Sam saw the muscles tighten like ropes in the brown back of the Sioux who lay at the base of his rock. The frightened mules were heading straight toward him. They were not fifty yards distant. He could see the young driver tense in the seat, boot on the brake, hands tight on the taut reins.

The man was so near that Sam could even make out

his fear-distorted face, a face he had grown to hate four years before at Fort Fred Steele: Corporal Bootle who had driven young Sam from the army with his envy and arrogance. Bootle was about to lose what hair he still possessed to the Indians which the army was protecting from whites like him.

If Bootle had not been such a fat-headed fool, he would have swung his mules when the Indians made their first rush, and tried to outrun them back to the main train. Down here, with his kicking mules tangled up in brush, with his ambulance halted, even upset, Bootle would not have a chance.

Singin' Sam Sling hated Corporal Bootle very heartily. Of all the soldiers he had encountered, Bootle would have won his vote for the booby prize. But when Sam Sling looked upon the puffy terrified face of Bootle, he ground out a curse, jerked his six-gun, and dropped off the top of his rock.

He hit the Sioux warrior so crushingly that he drew only a grunt. For the moment Sam felt his knees against the earth on each side of the Sioux, his crotch pressing down on the warrior's backbone. He hammered him in back of the ear with the barrel of his Colt.

Sam felt all the life go out of his victim as he sat astride the quivering body. He waited a moment, finger on cocked gun hammer for another warrior to jump him. They hadn't heard. They were watching the runaway mules, licking their lips for the hot blood of Corporal Bootle. The ambulance struck a rock and lurched over. The mules began to kick and fight in the harness. Bootle scrambled like a fat June bug toward the nearest cover.

And then above the pounding of hoofs and the snap and rattle of iron and wood and leather, Sam heard the clear scream of a woman. So Bootle had had a passenger in the ambulance. A white woman.

Sam Sling jumped off the body of the brave he had just killed. He went tearing down through the brush, his six-gun flaming as he flung lead into the front of the charging Sioux riders, rushing in to capture the ambulance, the mules, and passengers.

CHAPTER 6

The sudden appearance of the lanky mountaineer in dirty flapping buckskins, emerging from tall sagebrush on high lope behind a flaming six-gun, amazed the charging warriors. Sam's bullets were flying wild. He wasn't hitting any live targets for he was shooting to win time to reach the wrecked ambulance.

"Wagh!" whooped the leading buck, a sinewy warrior who had striped his face with green and black war paint. "Wah!" and he broke away to the flank less than ten yards from the ambulance.

The woman continued to scream as Sam charged in. The two mules were rearing and bucking, striving to kick their way free of the entangling harness. Two warriors, pressing closely behind their leader and half blinded by the dust kicked up by pony hoofs, reached the ambulance ahead of Sam. They arrived just as one of the mules broke an outside trace and whirled around to back away from his team mate. The sight and smell of the Indians drove the two mules entirely mad. The animal that had almost freed itself flung out its hind legs, and with the unerring aim with which mules are blessed, landed both hoofs squarely against the breast of one of the Sioux war ponies.

Squealing, walling its eyes, the pony went back on its

haunches almost hurling off its painted rider. The second buck, laying back on the line of his war bridle, striving to check his mount before he came in contact with the plunging mules, came within Sam's line of aim as he neared the ambulance.

Sam, figuring his gun had about run dry, let go and the Colt slug tore a hole through the bent back of the Sioux large enough for a man to push in a fist.

When the dead brave flopped off his mount, the immediate fight around the ambulance broke up. The war party that had fancied itself on the verge of taking pony soldier hair cheaply, scattered in four directions.

The tough hickory tongue of the ambulance which had until now withstood vast strain cracked like a fire cracker as Sam scrambled up and over the canvas side of the wagon. When the tongue broke off, the mules were finally released. They bolted deeper into the sagebrush, dragging with them remnants of harness and double trees. The Sioux fighters, who had been in hiding, waiting for their mounted friends to drive the team into their trap, rose up and began to snap whizzing war arrows at the mules. One animal went down as full of quivering arrows as a pin cushion. But its mates, somehow unhit, went kicking and plunging on through the brush.

Sam, finding a canvas curtain rolled up, thrust his long legs into the ambulance, intending to find cover inside the vehicle. Given a couple of split seconds, he figured he'd have time to reload the hot smoke-blackened Colt.

Another screech of fear from the woman he had saved deafened him. He turned his head and found himself staring down into a smudged face surrounded by a tumbled wealth of shining chestnut hair. She raised her head through the opening in the side of the ambulance.

A Sioux war arrow, flying wild, hissed past Sam's ear. He planted his left palm on top of the woman's head and gave a hearty push.

"Stay down!" he yelled, "Stay down! For Gawd sakes, quit screechin' like a hoot owl!"

He broke open his hand gun, raked shells from his belt, and began to reload. One empty shell was so hot it jammed. He jerked his skinning kife and got the edge of the blade beneath the rim of the shell, but the blade slipped out. He dropped the knife, deciding not to waste time attempting to extract the empty. But when he attempted to snap back the cylinder, the contrary rim blocked the action. Given a few moments of time, Sam could easily enough have cleared the cylinder and reloaded the gun.

But here in a hot and panicky fight, with war arrows whirring through the air, crazily yelling Sioux trying to kill a bucking mule, Sam wasn't able to think or move calmly. He knew that he was caught without a weapon for the defense of the woman and himself unless he could recover the knife which he had dropped. He wished that he hadn't laid the old Henry down on that hot rock. He had lost sight of the corraled wagon train and the Sioux riders. He was watching the Sioux who had jumped from the brush to grab the stampeding mules. He saw the kicking body of the animal that had been filled with arrows. He saw a Sioux buck make the vast mistake of attempting to seize the trailing bridle rein of the wild-eyed mule still on its feet.

The buck jumped like a jack rabbit toward the mule's head. He got a close grip on the bridle headstall. The mule reared back, letting out a sort of strangled bawl, whipping the buck off his moccasins and so high into the air that his breech cloth floated like a flag in the Wyoming breeze.

The mule began to rear back through the brush, shaking its head madly, striving to free itself of the clinging weight of the Indian. The buck would not let go of the headstall.

But then, and with a dreadful suddenness, the Indian dropped the bridle rein. His paint streaked body went limp as a dish rag. He flopped down over the top of a tall sagebrush and hung there, feebly kicking his legs. From the top of the butte came the boom of a gun.

At last Rocky Mountain Shorty had bought into the fight with old Susy. He had shot the Indian off the mule's head. But with black powder ammunition of slow velocity, and firing at long range, a man was apt to drop dead before the sound of the gun's report reached any observer's ears.

In the dust and smoke, Sam counted three Sioux afoot in the brush. When they saw their friend die so quickly, and heard the dull roar of old Susy, they all dived back into cover.

Sam looked around for Corporal Bootle, but couldn't spot where the fat driver had taken to cover. Now he would have time to reload his gun. But as he bent and began to fumble around inside the ambulance for the knife he had dropped, the stock of another hand gun was shoved into his hot hand.

"Here's one fresh loaded," the woman quavered. "I—I was saving it for myself!"

Sam looked down into her dirty face. He thought she would probably look younger and prettier if she could find time for a wash. But she had just come through the smoke and dust of Hell on the gallop and she could not be blamed for not looking presentable. He wasn't much of a judge of age in females. To Sam they were all either old or young ones. This one fell into the young class. From what he could see of her crouching body, she appeared like a good hefty sort, plenty of meat on her bones.

"Tarnation," he snarled, angry that she hadn't passed him the gun sooner. "Coulda took some more Injun hair if you hadn's been so worrit about yourself!"

Greenhorns always took stock in tall stories about women saving the last bullets for themselves in an Indian fight. Of course, if the men were captured, quite likely they'd roast over a slow fire. But Indians seldom killed any young or pretty women they captured. They carried them off to camp and trained them to skin out buffalo, pack wood and water, and help out their squaws. Sometimes they married them although a lot of Indians didn't think fragile white women classed up with squaws.

"I—I couldn't have stood it," the girl half sobbed, "if—if those fiends had caught me."

"Shoulda figured on that when you headed up the Bozeman Road to Montany."

"But—but we were going west to the Wind River country. To the Sweetwater mines."

Sam opened wide his eyes in amazement. "You're a good sixty miles off that road," he said. Then he decided that she was lying to him and that angered him. "Fools like you," he growled savagely, "would do most anything to pick up some of those gold nuggets in the Black Hills or Montana." He had encountered gold-crazed newcomers to the west who actually believed they could pick gold off the surface of the ground like a chicken picking up grains of feed.

His angry voice acted on the girl like a cold drink of water. It stirred her wrath and drove the fog of terror from her mind. She pushed up at his side, and her eyes were now almost on a level with Sam's. He saw that she was indeed a tall and mightily well developed girl. She was wearing some sort of a blue gown of light fabric. Rolling around in the ambulance when it overturned, she had caught her sleeve on a nail and torn off a sleeve. Her bare arm was round, white and supple.

The sight of that satiny white female flesh sent a queer little thrill through Sam Sling's weary bones. This was the first woman he had laid eyes on for more than a year. The girl's eyes were a sort of deep and flashing blue. When he talked rough to her, she had gotten up her dander. He grinned and licked his sun blackened lips.

"You—you," she gasped, backing away from him, "you grin just like a wolf."

"I reckon," drawled Sam, "I smell like one too."

He hadn't been watching the girl all this time. A man couldn't keep his eyes in one place while Sioux were roving around. But he saw that the Sioux had either quieted down in the sagebrush or pulled out. The painted riders, foiled in their effort to take the ambulance, had retreated to the rough hills. Sam now turned his head and looked up the long valley toward the train.

The wagons still stood in a rough circular corral. He heard guns popping now and then like distant firecrackers at occasional Sioux horsemen who appeared on the eastern ridge. But the main fight had been beaten off.

Toward the wrecked ambulance came a bunch of galloping horsemen. They wore the army blue. Several were riding on mules. At last the army had sent a rescue party out.

"About time," Sam grunted. "Danged coffee coolers!" He began to look around the immediate surroundings. "Where's Bootle?" he asked.

"Bootle?"

"That fat fool who was driving you."

"Oh—I thought you meant the other soldier. The—lieutenant down here inside the ambulance."

Sam's black brows went up. "Tarnation," he gasped. "You still got another soldier in this heap?"

"Look," she said, pointing downward with her bare white arm.

Sam'e eyes followed the motion of the arm. He found himself staring down into the interior of the ambulance. The flaring blue skirt of the girl's gown half hid the sprawled form of a man in a blue uniform. But Sam made out the yellow color of the stars on his shoulder stripes.

"A shave tail," he said. "A danged cavalry lieutenant. What's he doin' in here? Why isn't he out with the rest of those boys," and he gestured toward the oncoming knot of mounted men.

She had the grace to blush. "His name's Prime. Lieutenant Nat Prime. He's been quite polite since his men stopped our train. This morning he decided the ambulance should go ahead to stay out of the dust. And he'd ride with me so that he'd be on hand if we got into any trouble."

"He was a lot of help," Sam laughed.

"Anyway when your gun played out, I handed you his six shooter."

"My gun didn't play out."

"Well something happened to it. You were fumbling around there, looking wild-eyed, using foul language something awful."

"And you were screeching your fool head off. No wonder I busted up my gun action. That's what happens to a man out here when he gets tangled up with foolheaded females. Just like Shorty says. Only place fer women is in town. You can buy'em a drink, dance and have a good time with 'em. But leave 'em behind when you hit the trail. If you get lonesome fer women out in the short grass or the mountains, pick yourself a good sensible Injun squaw!"

"Oh!" she gasped. Her dirty tanned face turned the flaming color of a prairie fire. She drew back that graceful but muscular arm and slapped Singin' Sam across his mouth. "Classing me with a squaw!" she panted. This time she raked his astonished face with her finger nails taking away some of Sam's black whiskers. He reeled back, amazed, mouth wide open. They were at close quarters standing in the ambulance with their head and bodies forced up through the opening in the side. Sam couldn't easily dodge her blows. He did the next best thing. He wrapped his long arms around her and crushed her to his breast.

His arms filled with the struggling, gasping girl, Sam looked over her slim shoulders as the troopers began rolling off their ponies and mules. They were a nondescript outfit, in their dusty baggy blue pants with the tops stuffed into heavy socks, their feet clad in broad-toed army issue brogans. The majority wore blue fatigue caps. Their heavy blue shirts were gray with dust, and their broad red faces were grimy with trail dirt and powder soot.

Sam lifted up the girl and swung her clear of the wrecked ambulance. Then he released his grip on her muscular body. She slid down the canvas side to the earth. He climbed out the opening and hastily threw his moccasins on the ground. He was toting the lieutenant's six-gun at full cock, warily watching the soldiers. For Sam didn't know just what to expect from them.

The leader of the party, who had galloped up on a gray mule, hustled toward the girl and Sam. He was a sinewy sort of trooper, with a lank black mustache outlining his hardset thin lips. He wore a cavalry style slouch hat cocked on the side of his narrow head but Sam saw that the white chevrons and stripes of an infantry corporal decorated his shirt and breeches.

This amazed Sam since the unconscious lieutenant inside the ambulance, the shave tail called Nat Prime by the girl, was apparently from the horse branch of the army. It struck him as strange that a pony soldier should be commanding a detail of walkaheaps.

But he forgot his surprise when he took another look at the approaching corporal. Four years had passed since the old days in Fort Fred Steele but a man never forget the friends with whom he passed a few days in the guard-house after payday.

"Dillon!" he cried joyfully. "Spike Dillon!" Sam stepped forward, right hand extended and opened. There was a wide grin on his face. "What are you doin' away up the Powder? And ridin' a jarhead mule?"

Spike Dillon, concerned over the half weeping girl in the torn blue gown, stopped dead in his tracks as though he had been shot through the heart. His black eyes, as bright and hard looking as bits of badland soft coal, flashed a glance past the girl and toward Sam Sling.

"That voice," Spike said huskily. "I recognize it. But—but who are you behind all that hair and trail dust?"

These soldiers had come up so swiftly that many had not seen details of the fight around the wrecked ambulance. Some were carrying their long Springfield army rifles, the old .45-.70 caliber single-shot guns of Civil War days, at full cock. They hadn't failed to note the long blue pistol held by Sam. They knew all about this latest model of the Colt, and had a powerful respect for its mighty kick.

"Now see here, boys," roared Sam Sling. "Don't go to shootin' me up figurin' I'm a danged renegade that runs with war whoops. Spike Dillon here, knows me well. Many's the time I helped to sober Spike up after a payday. Why down at Fort Steele, once I toted him out'n Chicago Jack's joint after a card shark clipped him over his head with a pistol. Spike, tell these coffee coolers to sorta stand at ease while we line up on just what went on here."

Spike Dillon jerked his hard features into a black frown. "Sling," he growled. He never offered to take Sam's welcoming hand. "One of those Slings!" He stepped past the girl. "What you doin' away up here in the Injun country?" There was now deep suspicion in his harsh voice. He glanced hastily about him. "Where's the lieutenant?" he went on. "And what become of Corp'ril Bootle?"

Sam felt aggrieved that this man who had been one of his army bunkies should meet him after four years with hard eyes and harsh voice.

"Why, Spike," he complained. "I reckon Bootle's layin' around somewhere, maybe fainted or somethin' from his Injun scare. That shave tail from the cavalry is all laid out inside the ambulance. Me and this young woman—" he nodded toward the girl.

Spike cut him off sharply. "You're under arrest, Sling. Better lay down that gun!"

"Now listen here, Spike," Sam began angrily, rage beginning to simmer. "I'll lay down this gun when I danged please. The gal passed it to me when mine run dry. Them Sioux woulda got our hair shore if she hadn't. That's what happens when yuh depend fer any help from the danged army. What did you boys take so much time fer when the hostiles started yellin'? Did yuh have to stop and eat breakfast?" Sam was bearing straight down on Dillon.

CHAPTER 7

Sam's anger failed to daunt Spike. The corporal called to his men. "Keep him covered. If he tries to use that pistol, open fire." Then Spike repeated to Sam. "You're under arrest. Hand over your gun!"

Fear of arrest hadn't aroused Sam's anger. He had expected that, since he was caught deep inside Indian treaty territory. But what was an arrest between old army bunkies? What had come over Spike that he sized up Sam as though the latter were a mangy cur? It was enough to drive any simple-hearted mountaineer to the heights of blood red anger. Sam began to boil inside. He knew that in another second he'd run out all the loads in the lieutenant's gun, shooting it out with Spike and the doughboys.

"Spike," he said, between his teeth, "you haven't got enough men with you to get my gun! Any time you aim to try, cut loose your wolf!"

Spike, unafraid, held his grond. "For the last time," he said, "hand me that gun. Stock first."

"For the last time, Spike, come and get it."

They were not six feet apart. Spike carried a pistol in the holster on his cartridge belt. His blue-clad detail supported him, rifles held ready to open fire on Sam at the first hostile move.

It was the girl who broke up the coming battle. She stepped between Sam and Corporal Dillon. Her blue eyes were stormy. "This man," she told Dillon, "just saved me from the Indians. Also your lieutenant who's sprawled out inside the ambulance may be hurt bad. Why are you handling him as though he were a common criminal—a murderer? I handed him that gun which I took from your officer when he could not use it. To stop you men from a shameful killing, I'll take it away."

She swung on Sam, and held out her hand. He stood braced in his moccasins, breathing hard through his nostrils like a wind-broken racehorse. His thick black brows were drawn down over his smokey gray eyes in a frown. His gaunt jaws were set, his hairy chin thrust out like a saddle horn.

"If she jest touches him," one doughboy drawled to another, "she'll blister her hand."

"Use what horse sense you got," she said to Sam. "You can see you haven't any show against all these army guns. Hand over that six-shooter and tell your story to the lieutenant when he comes out of dreams. I'll back you up every inch of the way. If it hadn't been for you, we'd all be scalped this minute, me, Lieutenant Prime, and that fat corporal who doesn't know the first thing about handling mules."

Her calm talk took the edge off Sam's wrath. After all, shooting it out against a dozen rifles would be just more of the white brave courage that Tom Bear Mouth had derided. Sam smiled grimly but he bowed, and reversing the six-gun, handed it over, stock first, to the girl. Instantly, she turned on Dillon.

"Now you're safe from him. He's afoot. He can't run off. Hadn't you better take care of your officer? Also see what happened to Corporal Bootle?" She tilted her nose and sniffed. "Since you were a trifle late to fight

Indians, you can at least take care of your own men."

Spike's hard features turned red with fury. But he turned away and gave sharp orders to his men. They lifted the lieutenant from the ambulance, worked their way into the sagebrush where they found the groaning Bootle who had hidden behind a rock. One of the searchers also discovered the dead Indian with the cracked skull, and Sam's Henry rifle still resting on the rock.

A slug of cold water from a canteen revived Lieutenant Prime. He stood up rather groggily on his cavalry boots, rubbing a bump on his head as large as a sagehen egg. He was a tall, fair-haired young man, sporting a flowing cavalry style mustache. He wore his tawny hair rather long apparently styling himself after General Custer, the hero of the federal cavalry.

Prime's first concern was for the girl. "Miss Payne," he implored, "I don't know how to excuse myself for getting you into such danger. I never thought those accursed savages were so near." He turned on Bootle, paunchy and fat-faced upon sagging legs, supported by two grinning soldiers. "You," he said sternly, "who ever told you that you could drive mules? Letting that team run off at the first Indian yell. Why didn't you turn them back to the main train?"

"Now, Lieutenant," Bootle pleaded huskily, "I couldn't do a thing with those lazy mules. Them Sioux skeered them badly."

"A few days back," Prime answered tartly, " you had different ideas about mules. You classed yourself as an expert on mules before the board of review at Cantonment Sparks."

"But that was different, Lieutenant."

"Not much different. Another case of Indians frightening a man's mount."

"But he was riding a horse, not a mule."

Prime shrugged and turned to Dillon. "Corporal," he orderd, "have three of your men dismount. They will remain here, attempt to repair the ambulance. Bootle can stay with them. The rest of us will return to the wagon train and get under way."

Bootle almost wept. "Lieutenant, don't leave me here. Them Injuns may come back. I haven't got a gun."

"Pass him a rifle," said Prime. He bowed to the girl as a soldier led up a pony. "I hope I'm forgiven, " he murmured.

"You should thank this man here in the buckskin for saving us," she told him. "I don't know where he came from. But he arrived at the critical moment."

Prime nodded, turning to Sam. He thrust out his hand. "Sorry," he apologized. "I'm in your debt for the lives of Miss Payne and myself."

Sam grinned, shaking hands with him. "You're the first soldier in four years," he said, "who's treated me civil. That Spike Dillon there," he frowned, "he wanted to shoot me."

Prime turned on Spike but the corporal growled, "I was just trying to arrest him, sir. That's our order. Arrest all civilians found north of the treaty line without army passes. His name's Sling. Sam Sling. He's a mountain man. He hasn't explained yet what he's doin' up here."

"Sling," Prime scratched his head, flinching as his fingers touched the big bump. "You any relation to Sergeant Rick Sling?"

"My brother," said Sam.

Prime looked dubious, shook his head, narrowly regarding Sam. Then he sighed and went on. "I must place you under arrest as the corporal has explained. That's our orders from headquarters at Fort Fetterman.

My name's Prime. I'm commanding this detail of mounted scouts from one of our outposts down on the Platte. If you'll just mount one of these horses."

Sam nodded and mounted up. He felt glad that they hadn't questioned him closely about his business up here. He knew that Tom and Shorty were undoubtedly still up on the peak, watching all that went on. Doubtless they were discussing him heartily for getting involved in a fight with Indians and being captured by the army. He decided that if they questioned him again at the train, he'd swear that Indians had stolen some of his horses and he'd followed them north to recover the stock. If they didn't accept that excuse, he would just shut up and let them take him to the river and shove him south of the line. Shorty and Tom would soon show up around Canada Pete Narbo's trading post. They'd get fixed up and hit the trail, hunting for the Night Star.

As he jogged back to the train, he chatted with the soldier who rode at his side. He wanted to know about his brother, and news of the old regiment. He was informed that the first battalion had been sent north from Steele in the early spring to help guard the treaty line. Headquarters had been established at Cantonment Sparks on the river. Several outposts had been laid out to watch trails which trespassing whites might take north to Montana or the Black Hills. These mounted scouts were from one of the outposts located ten miles north of Cantonment Sparks.

Sam had to laugh. "Mounted scouts." He shook his head. "Half of you ridin' mules. What's come over the old infantry anyway? And a hoss lieutenant to command you."

"Short on troops," his guard answered. "Hard walkin' out here. So the army bought some Injun ponies and mules and mounted some of us up. That loot you met, he's from a regiment of hoss at Fort Laramie. Detailed on special duty to our outfit to instruct us in mounted scoutin' and the like."

"Tell him to keep his eyes open for Injuns usin' a lookin' glass to send signals," Sam suggested.

"He was inside the ambulance. That girl was keepin' him right busy. He's sweet on her."

"Miss Payne."

"Her hull name in Jane Payne. She owns most of that wagon train. Five wagons. Loaded with flour and grocery goods, she says, intended for the Sweetwater mines. She's a cornfed from old Missoury."

Sam rubbed his cheek ruefully where she had slapped his face. "She shore packs a cornfed wallop," he allowed. But he grinned. "I like 'em full of fight and vinegar. 'Course she yipped some at first but when she see how the game had stacked up and my gun had run dry, she shore fixed me up with Prime's hog leg." He could see Jane Payne riding ahead of the detail beside the lieutenant. Prime was bending from his McClellan saddle, very attentive to Jane. She was laughing. Out on the flank rode Spike Dillon. Sam's grin faded to a scowl when he spotted Spike.

"I'd like to catch him out in the sagebrush," he growled. "He's got pretty black eyes. But I'd make'em a sight blacker. Turnin' down an old bunky. One that dragged him out of Chicago Jack's deadfall down at Fort Fred Steele when we was bunkies."

"So you put in a hitch? What did you get? Bobtail?" the guard asked curiously.

Sam spat out angrily. "They gave me an honorable discharge," he snapped. "I put in a full hitch, I'd've re-upped if hadn't been for the fat Bootle. He was ridin' me. He hated my brother Rick, who was first duty sarge in the company ready to take over top kick when old

McNeal stepped out."

"So Rick Sling's your brother. Well he did get made first when the battalion came north."

"Good. I'll see Rick when we get to Cantonment Sparks."

"You may see him but you may not find it good."

Sam frowned. "What do you mean by that?"

The soldier shrugged. "Ask your old bunky, Dillon," he suggested.

Sam tried to dig out more information but his guard shut up like a clam. This worried Sam, this refusal to talk about his brother and the gossip of the battalion to which he had belonged. It seemed strange that his old friend Dillon had refused to shake his hand. More here, Sam decided, than a mere case of being arrested for trespassing on Indian land. He vowed inwardly that before another day came, he would corner Dillon somewhere and make him talk turkey or pound his Irish mug to a red mush. He was a civilian now. He could whip any corporal, even Bootle, without fear of being tried by an army court and thrown into the old stone mill.

Sam saw that the main wagon train was approaching, four mules dragging each heavy canvas-covered vehicle while bearded skinners sat on the high seats handling the reins and the brakes. Several horseman led the train. One who topped off a handsome black horse halted the train as the detail came up, then cantered forward to meet the soldiers. Prime halted his detail and rode forward with Jane Payne to greet the rider.

Sam squinted his eyes against the settling dust and the sun glare. That rider looked almighty familiar in his high black boots, his fringed buckskin hunting shirt, his long black hair that curled from beneath a wide-brimmed hat of cream color, creased down the middle.

He saw the nattily garbed horsemen bend gallantly in his saddle, and bow his head over Jane Payne's hand as she rode up beside him.

"Gah!" growled the soldier guard. "Kissin' her paw like a Frenchy. That Hacker's a devil with the women. Got some more along on this train that likes kisses."

"More?" snapped Sam. "You mean more than one white woman was fool enough to poke into war whoop territory."

The guard grinned. "Wait until you see the others. Sunset Liz and her two younger sisters, Dotty and Dolly."

"Sunset Liz. Why I've heard tell of her. She run a big quick lunch joint once in Cheyenne. When the town was boomin'." He saw that the rider named Hacker had turned and was escorting Jane Payne and the lieutenant back to the train. The name of Hacker touched up a chord in his memory of a smoky night in Fort Fred Steele, and a fight in a card sharp's dive.

"Hacker," he said, and swore. "That's his last name. But he's more generally known as Chicago Jack. What's he doin' up here with a bunch of women in his train?"

"Hard to tell what he has up his sleeve. That Payne gal claims he hired out to show'em a new trail to the mines on Sweetwater. She's got her guardeen along. An old pelican what calls himself Judge Barberry. They all swear they don't know they was across the line. Say they had heard grass was short on the regular trail to South Pass and Miner's Delight and they aimed to swing a little north and around the southern point of the Big Horns."

Sam swore. "Bah! Chicago Jack knows this range well as I do. He's been up here several times. No—he's got something else up his sleeve."

CHAPTER 8

Sam was given no opportunity to face Chicago Jack Hacker. For when the mounted scouts rejoined the main train, the caravan immediately resumed the long and tiresome return journey to Cantonment Sparks. Sam rode with the troopers but soon discovered that although several had served with him, none would talk to him as a friend. This fired up Sam's anger. As he jogged along, he passed the time framing another verse to his buffalo song that he hoped would sting the pride of his former bunkies.

The lieutenant commanded a noon halt at a water hole but allowed no time for boiling coffee. Horses and mules were watered. Soldiers grumbled as they ate their cold rations, consisting mainly of hard tack and bacon fried at their breakfast mess fire.

With nearly sixty miles to travel to the Platte, the lieutenant hoped to make the return trip in three days. Ordinarily this would have proved a killing pace for slow moving wagons but fear hung over the expedition that the hovering Indians would gather reinforcements and launch a full scale attack.

Sam watered the keg-headed pony with which he had been furnished, then picketed the animal on a forty foot rope to nibble the scanty grass. He planted his broad back to a tall sagebrush, and between bites into a sandwich of greasy bacon and hard tack softened up by being soaked in water, he sang for the disgruntled soldiery.

> *Oh take me back to the buff'ler days,*
> *When Injuns whooped in the prairie haze,*
> *Doughboys were half mules, half men,*
> *If they ever changed, Gawd knows when.*

Spike Dillon arose from a knot of his blue-clad mates with a murderous look on his face. He stepped over to Sam, and glared down into Sam's wide open mouth.

"Shut up your bazoo," said Spike, "Or I'll shut it for you."

Sam grinned and tossed aside the remnants of his lunch. He uncoiled his lanky body leisurely. He faced Spike, wiping bacon grease off his hands on the flapping outside seams of his buckskin pants.

"So you don't like my singin'," he jeered. "Well, here's another verse that might please you better."

He flung back his head and his twangy voice rose above the rustle of the wind in the sagebrush, and the confusion of the noon camp. Mule skinners sitting in the shade of covered wagons grinned and halted their eating to listen. At the head of the train, Lieutenant Nat Prime broke off his polite chatting with Miss Jane Payne and hurried back to where his men were stationed with their horses.

> *Oh take me back to the buff'ler days,*
> *When Injuns whooped in the prairie haze,*
> *Would fight right hard for a private's hair*
> *But passed up on corporals, I do declare.*

As Sam whined out the last word, Spike Dillon hit him, But Sam had expected that. He rolled his head with the punch, taking a glancing blow on his lean cheek. He blocked Spike's furious charge with an upflung left arm, then thrust back the angered corporal. Trained in rough and tumble fighting in many an army brawl, Spike saw immediately that Sam had lured him into a trap. He attempted hurriedly to get up his guard but before he could push his left fist into Sam's grinning face the mountain man swept his right fist up in an uppercut that popped off the point of Spike's chin.

Being a tough man, the corporal was not knocked out by the savage punch, but he reeled away from Sam, groggy in his boots, shaking his head madly to clear the fog from his brain.

Sam followed up mercilessly, swinging rights and lefts until his knuckles reddened with Spike's blood. He was cutting Spike's hard face to red rags, and jarring him from belt to collar button with punishing blows.

The corporal's fellow troopers, dropping hard tack and bacon fat, jumped up and crowded around the two battlers. Foremost in the ring was Corporal Bootle who had been picked up earlier when the train passed the wrecked ambulance.

Sam was enjoying himself, taking out all his ire against the army on luckless Spike Dillon. Spike would think twice before he ever again turned down an old bunky who had once befriended him in a tight spot. He pressed in closer to his weaving target, eager to knock him out for a full count. Spike's eyes were swelling shut. But he was a game lad. He stayed on his legs with his guard up although his knees were beginning to buckle.

"Pull that murderin' thief off Spike!" bawled Corporal Bootle, appealing to his muttering fellow soldiers. "He's tryin' to kill Spike! The dirty renegade!"

Spike pawed out blindly, seeking to close in and hang to Sam's body for a moment's breather. Sam padded around like a mountain lion in his soundless moccasins. He brushed away Spike's wavering fists. He snapped a punch to Spike's paunch. As the corporal fell forward, Sam stepped in and straightened him up with a sock to the chin.

The corporal's knees broke. He went down in a heap, still conscious but so weakened that he could not stay on his feet and fight.

Bootle, calling on soldiers to help the corporal, had ventured within arm's reach of the grinning bloody man he had called a renegade.

"Wagh!" roared Sam, giving a war whoop. He reached out and grabbed Bootle by the slack of his collar. He twisted Bootle's shirt about his neck so tightly that Bootle began to strangle and turn blue in his fat face. Sam held him with his left hand. With opened right hand he slapped Bootle, first on one fat cheek and then the other.

"I'm gettin' even," Sam yelled, "for the mules you couldn't drive!"

Bootle opened his mouth in a choked squawk which Sam shut off with another open handed slap.

But Sam was also keeping a wary eye on the remaining soldiers. They were crowding him closely. A half dozen hard men were there. Others were away from the halted train, holding a picket line against further Indian attacks.

Bootle's squalls and Sam's war whoops drew others to the fight. Bearded mule skinners hurried to the rear of the train where soldiers were circling around the battlers. Lieutenant Prime pushed impatiently past the grinning teamsters.

A woman thrust her head out of the rear of one of the

wagons. Her bright red hair gleamed in the sunlight. When she opened her mouth, she showed glistening gold work adorning her back teeth.

"Loot!" she cried out in a husky but not unmusical voice, "what's all the big noise about."

Prime shook his head angrily, never pausing to explain. But a huge mule skinner known as Red Dog, whose hair and beard matched the woman's in flaming red color, bawled out an invitation.

"Git your gals, Liz! Come on out! The doughboys is puttin' on a show!"

Liz grinned and nodded. She called out loudly, "Gals, we're missin' somethin'!"

Liz swung down from the rear of the wagon. She was a buxom woman, not young but boldly handsome. She wore a knee-length skirt. Beneath the edge of the skirt full Turkish pantaloons billowed. Liz wore striped red and white silk stockings on her shapely legs, and high button shoes with red tassels that had been rather badly dented and scarred up by rough travel on the trail. But she flashed a golden smile on Red Dog and his fellow teamsters, yelled to her girls a second time to wake up and see the show, and scurried down to the scene of the fight.

Her two girls Dot and Dolly, aroused by the shouts of Liz, crawled from the wagon rubbing sleep from their eyes. They were young and shapely girls, dressed in duplicates of the gown and Turkish pantaloons favored by Liz. As they followed after Liz and the teamsters, Jane Payne, escorted by Chicago Jack Hacker, overtook them.

"What's going on, girls?" Jane asked, in her breezy way.

Dot and Dolly sniffed knowing well enough that Jane did not fall into their class. Jane, an innocent from east of Cheyenne, took them as fellow settlers anxious to get a job as biscuit shooters in the restaurant of Sunset Liz in South Pass or Miner's Delight.

"Find out for yourself, Miss Money Bags," Dot answered rudely, shrugging slim shoulders and tossing her black curls.

"Ask that shave tail who's been sparkin' you," suggested Dolly, puckering her rouged mouth into a taunting smile, and patting her blond hair.

Jane frowned and started to reply. But Chicago Jack, stepping past her, gave Dolly a rough push to thrust her aside.

"Stand aside for your betters," Chicago Jack rapped out.

Dolly drew her painted lips away from her teeth. She slapped at Jack's face with a clawing hand and raked her nails down his smoothly shaven right cheek leaving a bloody trail.

"You hellcat!" Chicago Jack snapped, and took the blond girl by the throat. He shook her until hair pins rained from her curls and all her long blonde hair tumbled down around her shoulders. She screamed and kept on pawing at his enraged face. Dot, doubling her hands into small fists, whirled and attempted to rush Jack. Big Red Dog, rumbling with laughter, stepped in and seized Dot in his arms. He gave her a bear hug although she screamed and tried to escape. He silenced her with a smacking kiss.

Amazed at the fight that had so suddenly broken out between Chicago Jack and Sunset's biscuit shooters, Jane Payne jumped in and pulled Jack off Dolly.

"You should be ashamed of yourself!" she fumed. "Attacking a weak and innocent girl like Dolly."

Red Dog and his mule skinner mates roared with loud laughter. Chicago Jack took his hands off Dolly. She was weeping bitterly, cursing under her breath, seeking with fluttering hands to put up her hair and repair the bodice which Jack had rudely torn away, exposing her shoulders and a generous portion of her healthy bosom.

"Come on, Miss Jane," growled Jack. "Let's get out of here." He hurried on toward the scene of the main fight with Jane running at his heels.

"But why, Mr. Hacker," Jane panted, "did that girl talk about me and the lieutenant?"

"Because," Jack called back over his shoulder, "she's been tryin' ever since the train got stopped to get that shave tail sweet on her. If you wasn't along, she figures she'd have him wrapped around her pink little finger in a jiffy."

"Oh," said Jane. "I see now."

"Dot and Dolly and Sunset Liz," said Jack, "have been west for some time. You'll find out they got bigger ideas than runnin' a restaurant around the Sweetwater mines."

"But Liz has her wagon packed with a cook stove and dishes and things."

They were approaching the dusty howling knot of men around Sam and the two corporals he had taken on. Chicago Jack, regaining his good humor, scrubbed the blood off his cheek with buckskin glove, and said to Jane, "Liz can cook pretty good. But those Sweetwater boys will pay high for the favor she dishes out."

"Oh," whispered Jane, and asked no more. For just then the ring of men opened up and she saw Singin' Sam standing braced on his moccasins, choking Bootle, and slapping the fat corporal until he whined like a half-grown puppy.

"This!" roared Sam, "is for hidin' out when them Sioux tried to jump that Payne gal!" and whack went Sam's hand on Bootle's bulging cheek. "This," Sam went on, using the other hand, "is fer good measure! Runnin' the risk of lettin' a good lookin' cornfed Missoury gal lose her pretty hair!"

"Oh," cried Jane, and put her hands to her flaming cheeks, "Cornfed! Oh!"

She saw one of the soldiers whip up his rifle and cover Sam.

"Take your hands off Bootle!" the doughboy yelled. "You murderin' renegade! Take your hands off him!"

But before Sam could obey, Jane saw Chicago Jack Hacker whip a six-gun from his holster.

"It's a fair fight," drawled Jack. "Don't none of you walkaheaps buy in."

CHAPTER 9

Lieutenant Prime, breaking into the ring, checked the gunfight that threatened to flare between smiling Chicago Jack and the angry doughboys. He ordered his men to return to their duty. "Keep your eyes peeled for Indians," snapped Prime. "We've already lost our ambulance and a good team of mules because you were all asleep on duty."

Sam sped Bootle on his way with a swift kick in the pants. Spike Dillon was picking himself up from the earth, a bleeding wreck of a soldier. Prime swung angrily on the grinning mountaineer.

"What's the meaning of this?" he snapped.

"Just what you see, Lieutenant," drawled Sam. "Had to whip two corp'rils."

"Don't you know you're under arrest for trespassing in Indian treaty territory?"

"I had sorta got the impression I was held fer murder, the way them doughboys turned me down. Men like that Dillon that I soldiered with." He nodded toward Spike wiping blood off his battered face with a dirty neck scarf.

Prime nodded. "That's right," he answered. "I forgot! You're one of those infantry Slings, aren't you?"

Something in Prime's sharp voice made Sam bristle.

"And what's wrong with the infantry Slings?" he asked, advancing on the stiff young lieutenant.

But Prime wasn't a man who could be easily bluffed. He never gave way an inch to angry Sam.

"Nothing wrong with them so far," said Prime. Then he went on curtly. "If you don't stop this brawling with the soldiers of this train guard, I'll put you in irons."

Chicago Jack and the teamsters were watching and listening closely. A mutter ran through the dusty whiskered gang when the officer spoke of shackling Sam. But Prime turned sharply on them.

"Don't be fools," he said. "We have no time for brawling. We're three days from the river. There's plenty of Sioux watching us. Let's try fighting Injuns, not each other."

Sam, still bitter at the treatment he had received from the army, refused to be shamed by Prime.

"I thought," he jeered, "that it was now army policy to pet these danged war whoops instead of tryin' to kill 'em off like most of us want."

"You thought wrong," Prime said shortly.

"You and your soldiers are stoppin' American citizens from headin' north from the Platte to the Black Hills or to Montana. Ten years ago, the Bozeman Road was open and trains was halfway protected from war whoops by soldiers."

"You are familiar with the present situation, my man. You know that this territory between the Big Horns and the Black Hills has been turned over to the Sioux by federal treaty. You know that you are not permitted to go north of the line of the Platte without official permission."

"Don't call me your man," Sam spat out. He stepped in closer to the officer. They were about the same height and weight. "I been my own man for the past four years since I took my discharge. I can shoot off my bazoo all I like to any corp'ril or green shave-tail that hits this range."

Sam had enjoyed his fight with Spike and Bootle so much that he had grown careless. Prime hadn't been long out of West Point where cadets are trained to a fine point in the art of self defense. Sam was grinning through his wiry whiskers as he talked to Prime. But he quit grinning and went down on his back when Prime snapped a quick jolting uppercut to his chin.

"You can shoot off your bazoo so long as you don't pick out the wrong man," said Prime, standing over Sam. "I owe you plenty for saving Miss Payne. But there are limits to what I'll take off a dirty skulker who apparently hates the army." He stepped away from Sam, calling over a soldier.

"Stand guard on this man," he ordered. Sam was scrambling up with a black scowl on his face. "Keep him away from the mounted scouts! Find him a wagon to ride in. And you ride with him. But don't talk to him. You understand your orders?"

"Yes sir," answered the brawny, moonfaced soldier.

"Your name is—" Prime enquired, frowning because he knew that he should have known this private's name without asking.

"Private Huffenberger, sir."

"Ah— How much service, Private Huffenberger?"

"Six months, sir."

"A recruit, hey? Well, you don't know this prisoner at all. If he tries to talk to you or any other soldier, stove in his head with the butt of your Springfield. You understand?"

"Yes, sir," Private Huffenberger said, and gave

Prime the rifle salute when the lieutenant had stepped away from him.

Sunset Liz stepped up to Singin' Sam. She flashed him a smile and said in her sweetly husky way, "Sling, you can ride with me and the gals in my wagon."

Sam ran his eyes over the costume of Sunset Liz, the flaring skirt of scarlet, the puffed out pantaloons above red and white stockings, the tassels dangling from the high button shoes.

"Gosh," he gasped. "Where did you hook on to such a rig, Sunset? Last time I see you in Cheyenne, you sported a velvet gown with a train that looked tuh be ten feet long. Enough gown, I declare, tuh build a wickiup for three Injuns."

"Go on with you, Sam Sling," laughed Liz, digging Sam in the ribs. "Last time you were around me in Cheyenne, you and Rocky Mountain Shorty weren't able to see whether or not I even had on a gown!" She shook her red head gleefully." You two boys sure put on a big blow that time. Buckets of wine. Why, Sam, don't you remember how you was singin' and drinkin' wine out'n one of my satin slippers. Sam, I wouldn't forget a friend. You can ride comfortable with me and the gals!"

Sam was scratching his head, trying hard to think just what he had done on the big spree with Shorty last year in Cheyenne. He caught the round amazed eyes of Miss Jane Payne upon him, and he attempted to pass off the encounter with Sunset Liz.

"You sure are togged out for the trail," he told Sunset Liz, admiring her pantaloons and the shapely legs so generously displayed. "But—but ain't you apt to stampede your mules with them—them things you're sportin' so bold?"

Liz flung back her head and laughed loudly, showing

her gold teeth all the way back. Then she hit Sam so heartily in the short ribs that he almost lost his wind. It was all in good fun.

"You sure an ig'runt cuss," chortled Liz. "Didn't you ever here tell of bloomers? Invented by a right sort named Amelia Bloomer. She's so smart and so hot on equal rights fer women, that she aims to run fer president of these here United States."

"Hooray!" Sam cheered. "She gets my vote you can bet your stack. And Shorty's too!"

"Where is that sawed-off little hell raiser?" Liz asked. "Layin' out in the brush somewhere, drunk on Pete Narbo's trade whiskey?"

Sam figured he had talked enough with Liz. So far, he hadn't been questioned too closely about his sudden appearance when the Indians jumped the ambulance. He decided that Shorty and Tom had backtracked off the peak the moment the train and the soldiers had driven off the Sioux. They'd be hiding out. Come dark, they'd make time hitting for the river with their horses and pelts. They would be cursing him out for getting himself taken by the army. They'd not thank him at all if he squealed that they had been trespassing in Indian territory.

"Been a long time," he said cautiously, "since I seen Shorty drunked up on Pete's brand of rotgut."

Liz assumed that he meant he hadn't been partnering with Shorty for some time. She forgot all about Shorty. She took him by the sleeve and started off toward her wagon. But Lieutenant Prime interfered. He told Liz, with a twisted smile on his face, that while Sam might know how to conduct himself in the wagon of Sunset Liz, he could not risk Private Huffenberger.

"Huffenberger is quite new to the west and its ways," Prime grinned, "so he'd better find a seat for the prisoner in a wagon occupied exclusively by the male sex."

Sunset Liz cocked an eye of roguish blue and measured the big fresh-faced recruit.

"Why, Lieutenant," she said virtuously, "How you do go on? Why, I'd treat the big dutch-faced cornfed like a sister."

"I think it is better," the officer persisted, "for Sling to ride in some other wagon."

Liz nodded. She tossed a kiss from the ends of her fingers to Sam. She turned and ambled on past Jane Payne then called back to Sam. "Take care of yourself, kid. We'll have a pow wow when we get to the Platte. Some time when the danged army ain't stickin' its long nose into our private affairs."

Chicago Jack, holstering his gun, grinned at Sam. "That should be a real pow wow," he drawled. He called to the teamsters. "One of you boys can find a seat in your wagon for Sam Sling."

"He can ride with me," bawled Red Dog. "Any hombre that can whip two corp'rils can ride free with me any old day."

Sam answered cheerfully enough. "Whipped two corp'rils, Red Dog! But this here shave-tail walloped me." He winked at Prime. "When I wasn't lookin'."

Prime answered tartly. "After we get to the river, I'll be at your service any time. Until then, as a prisoner, you'll obey orders or get Private Huffen—er—get that private's rifle stock in the head!"

When Sam was herded past Jane Payne by strutting Private Huffenberger, he tried to halt and greet her. He was amazed at the blazing look she gave him from her blue eyes.

"Why—why what's come over you, Miss Jane?" he enquired, in puzzled tone.

"Cornfed!" she fumed. "So you consider me cornfed?"

"Well, you shore lean to the wellfed gitup."

Jane slapped his face.

"Hey!" barked the astounded Private Huffenberger, thrusting his rifle barrel and bayonet between the angry girl and the surprised mountaineer. "You can't attack my prisoner!"

"Take your old prisoner," Jane half-sobbed, " and give him back to the Injuns!" And she covered her eyes with her hands and fled from the scene.

Sam stood rubbing out the print of her fingers on his face, staring after her. "What's wrong about bein' a cornfed?" he wanted to know. "A cornfed's my idea of somethin' that shines."

Red Dog pointed to Private Huffenberger. "But she heard Sunset Liz call this dutch-faced rookie a cornfed. And also, she heard Liz snickerin' about you and Shorty puttin' on a spree with her. Looks to me, Sam, like that Missoury gal had gone plumb daffy over you and turned jealous. That's when you want to watch out. A jealous woman ain't responsible none. She's apt to bury a skinnin' knife in your back. Or bite off one of your ears."

Private Huffenberger thrust aside the teamsters.

"Stand away from the prisoner," he ordered in his thick important voice. He then told Sam to step out toward Red Dog's wagon. "And walk in step," cautioned Private Huffenberger, falling in at Sam's heels. "You've been in the army. Step out in time. Hep, Hep—"

Red Dog and his mates fell in behind Private Huffenberger in single file. They swung past the wagon from which Liz and her girls were watching and laughing.

"Hep, hep!" snapped Private Huffenberger, striding

along with his rifle at smart right shoulder arms.

"Hep, hep!" roared Red Dog, waving at Liz and the two girls. "Belly full of bean soup! Can't keep step!"

Sam strode ahead of Private Huffenberger, mixed of emotion. He wished to join in with the jeering teamsters. He knew they resented being run off Indian treaty land by the army. Unconsciously falling into a swinging infantry marching pace, he also found himself resenting civilian sneers at the army, particularly at the infantry branch. Huffenberger might be a raw recruit but he was only doing his duty. Half of a mind to turn around and bid Red Dog to shut up, Sam glanced off to his outer flank. What he saw, out in the distant sagebrush, made him forget present troubles. On a distant ridge he marked a man who had just dismounted from his pony. The man's blue uniform shone in the sunlight, informing Sam that he was a soldier. The man in blue was raising and lowering his rifle over his head. It was a familiar infantry signal to Sam Sling.

CHAPTER 10

Sam's shout of alarm was echoed almost instantly by the crack of a Springfield army rifle by one of the guards walking post a few paces from the train.

"Turn out the guard!" the sentry barked. "Turn out the guard. Enemy in sight!"

Private Huffenberger stood with a gaping jaw, gazing wide-eyed toward the distant picket who had sent the warning signal. The man had remounted and was galloping down through the sagebrush toward the train.

Red Dog and his fellow mule skinners, some cursing the Indians bitterly, scattered toward their teams and wagons. An army bugle began an insistent blaring of the assembly call from where the reserves of the train guard had eaten the noon meal.

Sam whirled around, and without another word of warning, raked the bayonetted rifle from the hands of Private Huffenberger. He snapped open the breech block, assured himself the gun held a shell in the chamber, then padded out to where blue-clad guards were bunching up in a thin skirmish line, all gazing toward the oncoming horsemen.

On the distant ridge so lately occupied by the galloper, a hand mirror began blinking flashes of light.

"Signals," Sam snapped as he came up to the line of

guards. "Sioux talkin' across this valley."

The train had make its noon halt in a wide valley bounded by mountain foothills on the west and the ominous bare ridge to the east. On this latter ridge appeared the enemy.

They would never be mistaken for white men. They were so far distant that even the color of war ponies was dull. But the free and easy way in which the men on the ridge rode back and forth, now bunching up, then fanning out into a skirmish line, indicated to all experienced plainsmen with the train that there rode the wild cavalry of the west, the warring Sioux.

"Signals," growled the soldier who stood beside Sam. "What they sendin' signals for?"

So engrossed were the doughboys in watching the approach of their mounted scout that not one had glanced toward Sam as he ran up, trailing Private Huffenberger's rifle.

Nor had Sam taken time to look over the line of soldiers. All were alert, fearing that any moment a knot of whooping red riders would dart from the brushy mouth of some hidden coulee, and cut down the gallant horseman who had signalled that the enemy was coming into sight.

When the surly guard spoke up, Sam glanced at him and gasped, "Spike! Spike Dillon!"

Spike turned his puffy face toward his late opponent. "Sling!" he called out. "Sam Sling." Then seeing the rifle in Sam's hands, he blinked his bloodshot eyes that were half hidden by folds of bruised flesh. "You're armed," he barked. "Where did you get a gun? Where—"

Sam started to explain that he had jerked it away from the hands of a startled recruit. But he knew that serious charges would be preferred against Huffenberger if the army discovered that he had allowed a prisoner to disarm him. It hadn't been Sam's thought to send poor Huffenberger to the guardhouse. But he had been trained to reach instantly for the nearest gun at the first alarm that the Sioux were coming. And Huffenberger's Springfield had happened to be the handiest weapon. Of course, a veteran of Spike's caliber would have shot Sam to death before he would have surrendered his weapon.

"We were up in the wagon when I saw the signal," he told Spike. "Huffenberger was getting settled around. I grabbed the gun and jumped out before he saw what I was doing."

"Hand over that gun!" Spike ordered menacingly. "You're under arrest!"

Sam backed away from Spike, readying the rifle, setting the hammer at full cock. He looked dangerous to Spike Dillon. The sight of Indians was like a sniff of potent war smoke to Sam Sling.

"Fergit that red tape," he said, between his teeth. "You fool! There's probably Sioux in the hills on both sides of this train. That's why the signals are bein' flashed. They may jump us at any minute from both flanks. We'll need to bear down with every gun available."

"You Injun lovin' renygade," Spike spat out. "You only got one bullet in that piece."

"I got a bay 'nit on the barrel," growled Sam. "If I miss with the slug, I'll give you the long thrust through your gizzard!" His smokey gray eyes carried a red look. His coarse black hair was blowing in the wind. As he talked to Spike, he kept on backing up, for Spike also carried a bayonetted rifle, and a pistol on his cartridge belt. Sam wanted to get enough space between Spike and himself for the thrust and parry of bayonet fighting if Spike went through with his threat of disarming him.

After the first alarm, the wagons of the train had moved hurriedly but without confusion into shaping up a corral for a barricade against Sioux slugs and arrows. Red Dog and his mates were all experienced in such maneuvers for they earned their bread by driving their outfits through hostile Indian country. Each driver, once he had taken up his leather lines, shouted to his mules and followed the wagon just ahead. At a shout from Chicago Jack Hacker, the captain of the train, the lead wagon turned and made a wide circle. When this had been completed, each wagon halted with its teams turned inwards. Drivers hurriedly freed nervous braying mules from the traces and herded them in the center of the circle. Men were appointed to watch the stock. If war arrows, flying over the tops of the wagons, wounded mules and threatened to stampede the stock, these guards would shoot down the injured animals to quiet the panic.

Where spaces intervened between the wagons, tongues were straightened out and set up on single trees to serve as obstacles against red horsemen who might attempt to ride through these spaces into the heart of the barricaded train.

Each wagon carried a huge wooden keg on its side for spare water. These would be opened and the water used if the Indians attempted to fire the train by shooting flaming war arrows into the canvas covers.

All this maneuvering took time but not as much as if the teamsters had been greenhorns. Every man worked without haste but made each move count. Gone was the gaiety with which they had mocked poor Private Huffenberger. All knew now that tardiness could mean death.

Sam hadn't wasted a thought or a glance on the train. He felt satisfied that men like Chicago Jack and Red

Dog would complete the barricade without difficulty. The present concern was to establish an outside line of skirmishers, ready to break any Indian charge with volleying Springfields if the Sioux launched an immediate rush.

But here was Spike Dillon, bitterly resentful because he had been mauled by Sam's fists, intent on his own narrow aim of disarming a prisoner, forgetful of the greater danger which now loomed.

"By Gawd," Sam swore to Spike. "If you don't get into line on the jump and be ready to shoot up the Sioux, I'll kill you if I hang for it at sunset. Are you rememberin', you fool, that we go some white women along in this train?"

That touched Spike Dillon to the heart. Every plainsman and veteran soldier worried more about women than themselves in Indian fights. It was popular talk that the fate of female pale-faces captured by hostile war whoops, was far worse than death. Women were always given guns before a battle and warned to save the last bullet for themselves.

Spike frowned but he lowered the point of his bayonet. He stood glowering a moment at Sam. Then he growled, "Turn in that gun after the fight!"

"Sure," said Sam. "What would I do with the blamed thing then?"

Spike nodded. He snapped a half dozen cartridges from his web belt with practiced fingers, handing them over to Sam. "We may need to fire more than one volley," he said. "You'll need spare ammunition."

Prime came jogging through with dust on his boots. His face was flushed with excitement but he was steadying his line of men with a calm voice.

"Spread out," he ordered, trotting along the line. "Each of you take cover behind a rock or sagebrush.

Don't fire a shot until you hear the bugle call of 'Commence firing.' After one volley, start dropping back to the wagons."

The lieutenant saw tall Sam hunting around for a buffalo wallow to hide in. He halted, with a frown on his face.

"You're a prisoner," he said, "but you're armed."

"Until things settle down," said Sam. "Then you can have your gun back."

Prime seemed to take Sam's promise at full value. He nodded and hurried on. The mounted scout now arrived, pulling down his froth-mouthed pony sharply, lurching off his McClellan saddle with a wisp of salute to Prime. He turned and pointed to the distant ridge where the Sioux were scattering.

"Whole pack of them on the other side," he said hoarsely to Prime. "At least fifty, lieutenant."

Prime nodded. "Glad you got in safely, Hobson. Take your horse inside the train. Then rejoin this skirmish line."

Sam, now flat on his belly behind an ant hill, turned and gave Spike a grin.

"Fifty of 'em he says. Supposin' there's fifty on the other flank. Ought to build up into a real scrap."

"We'll stop 'em," growled Spike. "A dozen soldiers and as many mule skinners, all armed with modern rifles against Sioux packin' bows and arrows, and some old smooth-bore trade guns. It'll be like shootin' ducks."

"Yeah," Sam drawled. "I've been around ducks that was danged hard to shoot. You're forgettin', Spike, that you soldiers have single-shot guns and some of these war whoops are beginnin' to pick up magazine rifles. Henrys and Winchesters. They pay high for 'em, I've heard. A pony load of beaver or buffalo for one gun or a box of fixed ammunition."

"You ought to know," Spike said, showing his teeth in

a nasty grin. "We hear at the Cantonment that you mountain men are makin' more money this year sellin' guns and shells to Injuns than tradin' with 'em for pelts, and usin' trade whiskey and beads and such gimcracks to close your deals."

Sam answered hotly. "If we wasn't settled down to line off the Sioux, I'd black your eyes again for that, Spike. Us mountain men got little use for a soldier but we don't go so far as to help the Sioux butcher 'em."

"You and me," Spike rejoined as heatedly, "don't agree on a hell of a lot of things. When we get this train to the river—if we ever do—I'll try to beat out your brains, Sam Sling."

Sam took another long look at the Sioux warriors on the distant ridge. Now they were riding slowly down the slope, coming toward the train. He could hear the distant thud of pony hoofs against rocks, the hoarse chant of the warriors as they sang some sort of a war song. The sky was filled with big white fleecy summer clouds that occasionally passed over the sun. But suddenly the sunlight slanted, outlining the Sioux riders.

Sam counted a dozen warriors in the fan of war. Their paint and riding gear flashed and sparkled in the sunshine. They had taken particular care to paint up for this occasion. That puzzled Sam. They were not resorting to usual Sioux attack tactics. Riding down slow that way. Singing their songs. Holding in their head tossing ponies with taut buckskin war bridles.

The playful Wyoming wind tossed the dyed eagle feathers that fluttered from the lance heads carried by the Sioux. The singing grew louder.

"Hagh!" the Sioux chanted. "Hagh! Hagh!"

"You get any of their danged lingo? Spike asked.

"Some. They are singin' that this is a fine sunny day to kick you pony soldiers outa their buff'ler country."

"If it wasn't fer birds like you," Spike said bitterly, "we wouldn't be here."

"Is that what you boys all hold against me," Sam asked curiously. "I figured I might get slung in the mill for jumpin' your fool line. But all you birds act like I had committed bloody murder, way you've been turnin' me down. Won't even tell me any news of the regiment or my brother."

He wasn't asking his old bunky for any mercy but in his heart, facing the oncoming Sioux, Sam was remembering when he had shared his blankets and pay money with Spike Dillon. Here, in the apparent start of a fight for life, he would have gone into it with a grin on his dirty face and ease in his heart if old Spike had held out a hand and told him to call quits to their feud.

Perhaps a similar thought touched the tough heart of Spike Dillon. For he looked at Sam with an instant of softness in his eyes. Then again they became hard and veiled behind swollen lids.

"We got orders not to talk to you," he said shortly. "You'll find out soon enough what all the row's about when you get to the river."

Sam shook his head. So they had not forgotten to question him closely about his reasons for being so deep into Indian country. From the officer on down the line, they were all under orders not to question too closely any prisoners they brought in. They were to deliver them at Cantonment Sparks where superior authority would do all the talking and questioning.

"There seems to be," Sam growled, "plenty of blood on the moon."

He wondered if some word of the fight in the beaver meadow had reached the army. Surely they would not be charging his friends and himself with murder for killing a couple of Indians. The law hadn't become quite so well established on the frontier yet that fights between whites and Indians were regarded as material for solemn jury trails and ensuing hangmen's gallows.

The army simply rounded up trespassers north of the line and kicked them out. If red or white men were killed, the army regarded that as just so much hard luck for the corpses.

"Wagh!" sang the line of Sioux warriors, shaking their lances and rattling their medicine gourds in time to the weird chant. "Wagh! This is our buffalo land."

"I ought to sing 'em a song myself," growled Sam.

"Save it," snapped Spike.

Sam grinned. He lined out his spare cartridges to his front so that he could reach them easily. He wished he had been given time enough to find his Henry and hand gun. But the army had taken away his weapons. These old Long Tom Springfields would tear out a man's belly at two hundred yards. But you had to reload after every shot.

CHAPTER 11

Except for an occasional bray from a fretful mule, not a sound came from the barricaded train as the Sioux approached. Every rifleman was in his place, some under the wagons, others in the spaces between, protected by whatever gear they could pile up that would turn away arrows.

The line of soldiers, flat on their bellies behind rocks and brush and ant hills—those chosen because soft sand stopped a bullet about as easily as a rock and wasn't so apt to throw off cutting rock chips if hit by a glancing bullet—kept their narrowed eyes on the painted warriors.

The Sioux came on until they were not fifty yards from the skirmish line.

Soldier fingers itched to press triggers. But discipline restrained them. They had been ordered not to fire until they heard the bugle.

Sam licked dry lips and whispered, half to himself. "They have let 'em come in too close."

Those swift little ponies could cross fifty yards before a man could draw two deep breaths. Half the skirmish line would fire, then reload hastily as their mates snapped a volley. But armed with single-shot guns, these soldiers were up against fearful odds with these swift and expert horsemen. Sam wondered why the army didn't equip its frontier troops with magazine rifles.

"More red tape," he snarled. "They got to lose a couple of regiments before they learn."

A man always learned to soldier the hard way in the west. Hard tack and fat bacon for rations. In lonely little outposts where supplies could not be hauled in during the winter, scurvy broke out, and men whose teeth were dropping from their shrunken gums, grazed like cattle when the first green grass and wild onions grew up in the spring. Treacherous white men sold the modern arms to painted warriors but the army continued to send its infantry into battle armed with the same sort of rifle with which battles had been waged in the war between the states.

"If I hadn't been took by the danged army while tryin' to stop a passel of runaway mules," Sam allowed, vastly disgusted, "I wouldn't run chances of losin' my hair today."

Spike growled, "If the army hadn't taken chances on letting you have a gun and spare shells, you might be losin' your hair without the chance to fight for your life."

"Well I sure do thank you boys for your kindness," jeered Sam.

He was examining the Sioux closely, seeking some warrior with a blue army blouse buttoned around his sinewy brown body. He was also looking for his stolen buffalo horse, and for a chief who rode on a yellow pony. He didn't think he'd spot the stolen Indian woman with the war party. They seldom let squaws accompany fighting men. Even when it came to their horses, warriors on raids never used mares.

But Sam saw something that put a spark of interest in his wary eyes.

"Hey," he called excitedly to Spike. "Those war whoops are actin' like pony soldiers."

"What do you mean?"

"Dang it all, man. You a corp'ril and supposed to know the book. Can't you recognize a flag of truce?"

He heard Spike slowly expel his breath. "Gosh," whispered Spike. "You're right. A flag of truce. Maybe—maybe this won't be a fight today."

These doughboys would fight to the bitter end but not a man there knew that they were badly outnumbered by the Sioux. More of frontier army methods. Never enough soldiers on hand to handle the situation. For all the big talk by the generals it was the tough blue ranks who were forced to back up words with action.

A white rag did indeed flutter from the tip of a lance.

A single horseman carried it. He rode out in front of the line of Sioux warriors as the painted cavalcade came to a halt. Advancing for a half dozen yards, he halted too. He waved the lance. The white flag fluttered into the gentle wind.

The horseman had come so near that Sam's sharp eyes recognized his squat body, slouched in a Mexican-style saddle, and the thick black beard that half masked his face. Sam cursed and spat into the ant hill, drowning a half dozen big black ants.

"You know him?" Spike asked.

"Sure do. That's Narbo. Canady Pete Narbo. I bought my winter grubstake from him last fall."

"What's he doin' with these Injuns? Is he a breed?"

"Don't know for sure. He comes from the north. Been tradin' with the tribes for years. Talks a half dozen lingos. Army uses him a lot as interpreter."

Canada Pete kept on vigorously waving his flag of truce. The Sioux had ended their war song. They were holding in their ponies, closely watching the train and its guards.

Prime stepped out in front of the skirmish line.

"Careful, lieutenant, " Spike called out.

Prime nodded. But he stook stiff as a poker, facing the Indians and Canada Pete.

"You're all covered," he called to Canada Pete. "I'll open fire if your Indians come a step nearer this train."

"They ain't my Injuns," Pete complained. "They brought me up from my tradin' post to talk to you. Killed a pony gettin' me here. Let me come in closer where I won't strain my voice."

"Come in alone," said Prime. "But tell them to stay where they are."

Pete turned and talked earnestly to the halted warriors. They nodded. He spurred up his pony and came in slowly until he had reached the waiting officer and the line of hard-eyed soldiers. The trader was a bulky man in his dirty buckskins and thick hair and beard. He wore an old slouch hat and knee-high moccasins.

"He hasn't got a rifle on his saddle," Sam whispered to Spike. "He may be tellin' the truth about the Injuns fetchin' up here for a pow wow."

"I don't trust nary white who's so danged intimate with war whoops," growled Spike. "If they try anything funny, I'll put my first bullet through the bright right eye of Canada Pete."

"I'll take that buck jus behind him," said Sam, "who'sall painted up fancy as a Pennsylvany Dutch farmer's barn."

Canada Pete, knowing as an experienced frontiersman that he had aroused the suspicion of the troopers, leaned from his saddle and talked in an aggrieved whine to Prime.

"I can't help bein' here, " he said. "You know me, lietuenant. I've done lots of things for the army. Cap'tin Budhouse trusts me. I hold a trader's permit from the army. It's like I say. A couple of these Sioux bucks routed me out at first dark last night. I'm rode down to a whisper. But they told me they wanted you to get word from their chief from a white man you could trust."

"Who is this chief?"

"He is called the Kicking Horse. He stands high in the Sioux nation."

"Where is he?"

"I don' know. Probably back in those hills where they got a pretty big camp."

"I'd prefer to see this Kicking Horse, eye to eye. He's already broken the treaty by attacking us."

"He aims," drawled Canada Pete, "to attack you some more, lieutenant."

"We're ready for him."

"But he wants me to tell you he won't waste warriors and ponies burnin' this train. He's callin' for help. He aims to make his big attack on Cantonment Sparks. He says he can bring a thousand warriors down to take the hair of all the pony soldiers."

"I think a battalion of infantry will prove that his aim was bad," Prime said dryly.

"Think what you like, lieutenant. I'm just deliverin' the message of Kicking Horse. He says the army has broken the treaty by letting white men go into the Big Horns and take Sioux beaver. He says when the Injuns tried to capture these trespassers your troops protected 'em. That Sioux were killed by soldiers while trying to run these trespassers out."

"The treaty states that the army shall handle all white trespassers. The chief knows that."

"Kicking Horse wants me to tell you," Pete persisted, "that right now you are holding one of these trespassers. There were three of them but two got away. He figures he can catch two of them. He says that if you'll turn over the man you caught, then he'll call off the attack on Cantonment Sparks."

Sam tensed up. So he was the center of this whole deal. The army, which didn't like him very much, could turn him over to Kicking Horse and halt the outbreak of another large scale Sioux war. Sam knew well enough what would happen to him if he was delivered to Kicking Horse. Rawhide Buttes got the name from a delivery of that sort in the early days. Indians could skin a man alive and take hours to do it. The inside of Sam's mouth felt dry and rough as cotton. For a long time he hadn't worried much about the arrow wound in his side but now he began to feel it again. Laying here under the hot sun, he could feel every inch of his lanky body. Never had that body seemed so dear to him as this minute. Never had the sun felt so warm and never had life seemed so sweet as it did now when Sam Sling lay on his hollow retching stomach and looked past Canada Pete into the impassive painted faces of Sioux horsemen.

Then Prime spoke, and shortly. "Go back and tell your chief—"

"Not my chief, lieutenant."

"Go back and tell this Kicking Horse that the army does not take prisoners just for the fun of turning them over to the Sioux. Tell the Kicking Horse to go out and catch his own prisoners."

"If I go back and talk like that, lieutenant," Pete whined, "he'll likely scalp me."

A new and hot voice broke into the pow wow. Chicago Jack Hacker loomed up suddenly at the side of Prime. Hacker's right hand was hard on his holstered gun. He glared up at Canada Pete. The interpreter seemed startled.

"You double crosser," snarled Chicago Jack. "You Injun lovin' double crosser! By the livin', I ought to shoot you off your pony."

Canada Pete stared down at the angry plainsman with a bewildered look on his bearded face.

"Now, Jack," he whined. "That shore ain't no way to say howdy to an old friend. You musta been drinkin' heavy."

"None of your mountain lion sweat," sneered Jack. "You know what I mean. It stands. I see now why the danged army stopped this train. You tipped 'em off. You was the only man knew which way I figured to head." He swung on the lieutenant. "I reckon that's why you overtook us."

Prime answered bruskly. "No time now to talk about that. Get back to your wagons. Our important business right now, is this pow wow with the Sioux."

Chicago Jack stalked angrily back to the train. He passed Sam Sling who was also watching Pete. Sam was recalling that Pete had outfitted his partners and himself the autumn before when they made ready for the Big Horn trip. The suspicion took firm root in Sam's mind that Pete had plotted the recent raid which led to the murder of Buffalo Hump and the loss of the Night Star. Sam determined that when the time was ripe, he too would see Pete again.

"Go back to Kicking Horse," Prime said to Canada Pete. "Tell him if he tries anything like raiding this train or the Cantonment, the Washingtons will send heap big bunch of walkaheaps and pony soldiers, even wagon guns, to fix him."

"I'd shore hate to see you give these reds a white man," Pete said soothingly. But he shook his shaggy head, gazing toward the train. "You're shore runnin' powerful chances of losin' your women to the Sioux."

"They must run their chances. They came up here as trespassers."

"Kicking Horse will be mad," said Pete, turning his pony.

Sam Sling slouched out, trailing the Springfield.

"Wait a minute," he drawled amiably.

CHAPTER 12

At sight of Sam, the Sioux to the rear of Canada Pete began chattering like a flock of enraged magpies. Sam grinned broadly and began to taunt them in their own lingo. He asked them what had happened to their strong war medicine? It seemed that one lone longhair could still whip a dozen of their best men. Perhaps they had better get back to camp and send the boys out to fight while they did work for the squaws.

Canada Pete rolled his eyes. "So you're the hombre they want," he said as though vastly surprised. "So I reckon the two that got away must be your pards, Rocky Mountain Shorty and Tom Bear Mouth, that Shoshone."

"Are you so danged surprised, Pete? And what's the latest St. Louis auction price on prime winter beaver fresh out'n the Big Horns?"

Pete licked his thick lips. "I don't know what you're drivin' at," he answered sullenly.

"Chicago Jack claims you tipped off the army to his train headin' north. I'm beginnin' to think you tipped off the Sioux to our camp in the Big Horns. You was the only white man that knew enough about our plans last fall to trail us into the mountains. You could let us get in a winter's trappin', spy on us, and when the time was right, get a big drag of beaver pelts."

"Now that's a danged lie," Pete said hotly. "If I wasn't tied up here on this pow wow business, I'd get off and fight fer such talk."

"If the army wasn't keepin' cases on me, Pete, I'd haul you off your war pony and make you fight."

Prime broke in angrily. "You two are holdin' up this train arguing like this."

Sam nodded, still amiable. "That's right, lieutenant. I just wanted to point out that I figure this Pete is a renegade. He's sellin' out his own blood to hostile Indians. I'd bet a bale of prime beaver that he hasn't been near the Platte River for the past four or five days. He's been up in the Big Horns, figurin' how to murder a good man so he can steal his wife."

With a snarling curse, Canada Pete came off his horse, snaking a bowie knife from his beaded belt as his moccasin toes hit the hardpan. He ducked his head and ran in on Sam, the knife point thrown forward in the hopes of ripping open Sam's lean belly. The army had taken away Sam's skinning knife but he was carrying a long rifle with a bayonet fixed to the barrel. He pitched the rifle forward, as Pete came in, and drove the bayonet through the slack of Pete's right sleeve. The furious trader struggled to free himself, cursing that no man could call him a renegade and live to boast about it. Sam held him off, laughing as he watched Pete's struggles.

At Prime's shout, soldiers rushed up and seized both men. The Sioux escort had become excited. They were crowding their nervous ponies nearer the train.

Prime roared. "First squad! Make ready! Prepare to fire!"

Up went the rifles and eight doughboy's sights covering the Sioux. The Indians heard the snick of gun hammers being cocked, looked into the black muzzles of walkaheap guns that could kill at a mile. Sullenly they backed their ponies.

"Corp'ril," Prime said to Spike Dillon. "Keep those Sioux covered. Open fire with your squad if they start anything."

Prime turned on Pete. "Mount up and get back to your chief with my message."

Pete rubbed his arm, gazing intently on grinning Sam Sling.

"I'm not forgettin' this," he threatened.

"Nor me," Sam assured him.

Pete thrust a moccasin toe into his wooden stirrup and mounted up. Sam noted that he went into the saddle Indian style, on the right side of his pony.

A soldier returned the bowie knife to the trader. Pete, with a last glare at Sam, began turning his pony.

"Wait a minute," said the mountain man. He turned to Prime. "Let's make this a real sportin' event," he said. "That Kickin' Horse seems to want me bad. And looks like the army figures I got 'em into this mess with a whole caboodle of female folks. Now here's my proposition, lieutenant. Loan me a fast pony. Give me my Henry rifle, shell belt, hand gun and knife and a hundred yards start on those war whoops. And Kickin' Horse can call off any attack on this train or Cantonment Sparks."

Canada Pete looked down and sneered, "White brave."

"Ask your pet Injuns," Sam persisted. As the trader sat silent, Sam began talking to the Sioux braves in sign and voice lingo. They returned no answer. He added taunts that they were Sioux squaws. Then he flung back his head and began to sing.

Oh take me back to the buff'ler days,
When Injuns whooped in the prairie haze,
But when the Sioux met a lone white man,
They turned their rumps and ran and ran.

He broke off his weird chant with more comments on Sioux styles of fighting. He was striking deeply at their fierce pride and their superstitious belief in their war medicine. He wound up by asking them what had become of the pony soldier's coat. And why didn't they play war music on the pony soldier's bugle horn? Was it still true that the Sioux of the Kicking Horse band had been sired by skunks and jack rabbits? If they were real men, and their medicine was strong, surely they'd gamble on being able to run down one lone white.

The Sioux would have ridden straight down on Sam if the army rifles had not held them back. They set up a wolfish yelping. And finally Canada Pete said to Prime. "They say its a bet. Turn loose this wolf. And there'll be no fight on your train or the Cantonment."

Sam laughed and said to the iron-faced lieutenant. "I'll go back and pick out a pony."

But Prime answered sharply. "You'll stand right here. The army does not require this show of heroism on your part." He turned to Pete. "This man is our prisoner. Tell Kicking Horse to come to the cantonment peacefully and the pony soldier chief will smoke a pipe and talk with him about this fight in the Big Horns. If this man who sings has shown a bad heart, the army will punish him by putting him in the big stone corral."

Pete jeered at Sam. "You and your fool singin'." He nodded to the officer. "I'll tell the chief, but I don't think it'll make his heart good. You better get set for plenty of trouble, lieutenant."

Pete rode slowly to his waiting braves. Sam watched him depart, a black frown on his face. He turned angrily on Prime. "I meant what I said. I wasn't tryin' to show off."

"Nobody accused you of that. You're our prisoner. It's our order to return you and these other trespassers to Cantonment Sparks for questioning by the commanding officer."

He turned to Spike Dillon as Pete and the Sioux rode slowly away through the sagebrush. "Deploy skirmishers until the train is hooked up. Then take your usual posts as advance, rear and flank guards. I'll be with the advance wagon."

"Yes sir," said Dillon. He nodded toward Sam. "What about this prisoner?"

"Disarm him and turn him over to Private Huffenberger." Prime frowned and looked around him. "Where is Huffenberger?"

Huffenberger stalked up. He was carrying a gun. It was Sam's pet Henry rifle. He snapped his heels together and gave Prime the rifle salute. The lieutenant noted that the private was not armed with the proper style of weapon. Sam cut in angrily before Prime could explode over the head of the luckless soldier.

"I grabbed his rifle away while we were climbing into Red Dog's wagon," he said. "The rookie couldn't help it. I was pretty scairt at the way you had told him to cave in my ornery head. I was tryin' to get away."

"Take him back," Prime said to Huffenberger. "This time see that he doesn't get away with your gun. Follow my former order. Cave in his head with the butt if he makes another funny move."

"Yes sir," said Huffenberger. He took back the rifle which Sam had jerked from his grip at the first sign of Indians. A grinning soldier passed it over. But now Huffenberger found himself vastly puzzled. He was carrying two rifles. Army regulations did not prescribe the manner in which a guard should carry two rifles.

"What are you waiting for?" barked Prime. He had turned away and was ordering the teamsters to hook up and string out.

"Which—which goes on the right shoulder," stammered Huffenberger.

Prime shook his head, then held out a hand. "Oh, give me that Henry," he said in a weary tone.

Huffenberger, relieving himself of the Henry, executed an about face, and marched Sam off to the train. As Sam approached the wagons, he saw the grinning whiskery face of Red Dog and heard the muleskinner's song.

Hep! Hep! Belly full of bean soup!
Can't keep step!

The mules were hooked up with many loud yells of "Gee" and "Haw." Sam sat in the high seat of Red Dog's wagon, baffled and angry. The train might be attacked and taken by Kicking Horse before it reached the river. Sam knew that as trespasser into Indian territory, he had aroused the anger of the Sioux. He had figured when he offered to outrun the Sioux, that he stood a fifty-fifty chance of saving his hair. He had been certain of one thing. If they overtook him, he would not be taken alive for their torture fire.

As the wagons lined up for the roll out, he could hear the chatter of Sunset Liz and her girls coming from the covered wagon that followed Red Dog's. The light female voices, the occasional giggles of Dot and Dolly, the musical husky contralto tones of Liz reminded him of the peril these women ran.

Even a visit from Sunset Liz didn't revive his spirits. She ambled up to the wagon and grinned at Sam. She was carrying a black bottle. She was sunburnt and dusty. Her silken bloomers had picked up stickers from the beds of prickly pear cactus that grew all around.

"Have a drink, camarado," Liz suggested, and held up the bottle. "You was a dead game sport to figure on outrunnin' them war whoops."

Private Huffenberger, sitting in back of Sam on a stack of cases and big wooden barrels, cut in. "Prisoner's not allowed to drink hard likker on duty."

"Now who said this was hard likker, sonny boy?" asked Sunset, winking at Sam. "This here is prairie cough medicine. I make it myself from an old family recipe that dates back to the days of Andy Jefferson. Sassafras an' sarsp'riller! And good grade alkali water. Here, soldier, if you don't believe what I say, try it yourself."

Huffenberger looked at the proffered bottle.

"Sam, here, is comin' down fast with gallopin' comsumption of the gullet. That's terrible catchin', soldier, out here in these dry hills. Man catches it, he's apt to cough up both his lungs. Take a slug of this brew. It's a sure cure fer whatever ails you."

Huffenberger uncorked the black bottle, tilted his bullet head, and put the neck between his lips. He took a deep draught. Sam could see the adam's apple jiggle up and down Huffenberger's fleshy throat. Then he saw Huffenberger's innocent blue eyes pop like those of a deep sea fish pulled suddenly to the surface. Straightening up he gasped out while tears began streaming from both his eyes. He nearly dropped the bottle.

"Hey!" yelled Liz to Sam. "Don't let the blamed recruit drop that bottle and bust it. Can't draw no more until dark comes on."

Sam took it and sniffed the contents while Huffenberger gasped and clawed at his throat.

"Trade whiskey," he told Liz. "I think I'll pass.

Ain't drunk nuthin' since last fall."

"It won't hurt you, bud. Not a heap big strong man like you. Good lookin', too, even if you got as much hair on your face as a grizzly b'ar." Liz looked up at Sam with languishing eyes. She said in a wheedling tone. "Let me know if you figure it'll go good with the boys in Montany."

"I figured you was headin' fer South Pass to open a cafay."

Sunset winked at Red Dog who had stalked up, trailing his long buckskin whip. "He talks almost as simple as that dutch-faced soldier," she said. "Now what fool would aim to set up for business in a blowed up camp like South Pass?"

To please a lady, Sam took a swig of Sunset's favorite pain killer. The fiery stuff burned him all the way to his toes. He felt as though he had swallowed a lighted candle.

"Gah!" he echoed Huffenberger, gasping for air as he passed the bottle down to Liz. She laughed and said to Red Dog. "What's come over these tough boys from the far back hills? You take a drag, Red Dog. You're a real authority."

Red Dog obeyed and drank deeply. Taking the bottle from his mouth he breathed deeply, returning it to Liz. He said, "I got a balky mule there on the left in my lead team. Don't want him to hold up this train, Liz. Let me give a slug to that mule and he'll sure take off."

"My tonic's too danged delicate for mules," said Liz. She threw a kiss to Sam. "Well, sonny, we'll finish this bottle when we hit the river. Until then—ta ta!" She swaggered off, wagging her shapely hips, and displaying her fluttering bloomers up to her knees.

Sam wasn't watching her departure. He sat in a stricken silence watching Jane Payne march past the wagon in a sort of frozen anger. Jane had flung back her head. She wouldn't look his way. But he felt sure she had seen him aparently flirting and drinking with Sunset Liz. Jane was being escorted by Lieutenant Prime, and a pudgy old gentleman with long stained gray mustache and goatee on his moon face.

"We should never tackled that stuff,'" coughed Private Huffenberger. "Takes a red-headed woman like Liz to make a fool out of a man."

"You said it all, soldier. But don't hold it down just to red-headed women." Sam gazed after the straight relentless back of Miss Jane Payne as she headed off to the head of the train, guarded by the old man and the very attentive handsome lieutenant.

Red Dog climbed up and kicked off the brakes. From the head of the train came a high-pitched yell: "Roool Out!"

Mule skinners cracked their whips and began talking loud blue mule language. Red Dog gathered up his ribbons and picked a fly off the long ear of his balky leader with his silk whip. Wheels began slowly to revolve as the mules put their shoulders against their collars. The train was under way, heading for Cantonment Sparks.

The soldiers of the train guard were vigilant. They lined both flanks, eyes ever turned toward the hills where the Sioux undoubtedly were waiting and watching. Three well horsed scouts rode in the advance. A strong rear guard was commandd by Corporal Spike Dillon. Chicago Jack galloped back and forth along the train, aiding teamsters who had trouble getting over high centers, keeping an eye out for Indians.

"You and me's agreed on Canady Pete," he said. "When we get to the river, maybe we can make a deal about him."

"Thanks," Sam said. He could not forget that this man had aided him in his time of need.

CHAPTER 13

By order of Lieutenant Prime, the wagon train made an early evening halt, formed its corral, and unhooked the mule teams. Under strong guard, the work stock was herded near the camp for grazing on the bunch grass. Fires were lit, the evening meal put on to cook. Prime passed out the word that when darkness came, the train would commence a night march. Camp fires would be built up and left burning to deceive any Indian scouts who might be watching from surrounding hills.

Sam ate his supper with Red Dog and two other teamsters. Private Huffenberger also received civilian rations which he received gratefully since they were of better quality than the march meal being served to his fellow soldiers. Chicago Jack dropped down by the fire for a bit of talk as the sun began sinking back of the western hills. Dusk was ushered in by the cooing of mourning doves and the flickering flight of graceful night-hawks.

Sam enjoyed his supper of mulligan stew of dried buffalo meat, strong unsweetened black coffee, and soda bread cooked in a frying pan. He knew Spike Dillon and his friends were dining on hard tack and fat bacon. Huffenberger bent so eagerly over the appetizing mulligan that Sam got in a few words of private talk with Chicago Jack.

Since joining the train, Sam had been curious as to why the train had gone far north into Indian territory while Jane Payne believed her wagons were being guided west to the Sweetwater Mining region which was open to pale face settlement and trade. Jack laughed about that when Sam made enquiry.

"Jane and her guardeen, that old jasper you see around here with the gray whiskers, they're greenhorns." Chicago Jack explained, laughing. "They brought out a big stock of groceries by rail to Cheyenne, then freighted up to Cantonment Sparks. Seems like the girl is an orphan and sunk all her inherited stake in the stuff. She went strong on flour as she had heard big talk of high prices in the minin' country. Hundred dollars a hundred weight for flour, twenty eight dollars for a small sack. Course she's got her sights set too high for Sweetwater where they can freight stuff in from the railroad durin' summer season."

"Flour and such would bring high prices in Montana," said Sam. "With the Bozeman Road closed."

"Yeah. I sorta pointed that out to the girl's guardeen, ol' Barberry. The old fellow was willin' to take a chance on Injuns if I'd guide the train north. So he kinda explained to Jane that we had to make a big swing north to find better grass along the trail fer our mules."

"And in so doin'," Sam said coldly, "you got turned back by the army and danged near massacreed by the Sioux. If that girl had lost her hair, Jack, you and her guardeen would be all to blame. That ought to be somethin' for you to laugh about now that this Kickin' Horse is ready to jump us any time he feels able."

"Now don't get sore-headed at me, Sam," Jack objected. "This ain't the first train that ever got north without bein' checked by soldiers or Injuns. Only reason you're puttin' up the big talk is because like most all us men you been makin' eyes at Miss Jane Payne."

Sam choked on his coffee. He set his tin cup on the earth and got up, ready to fight. But a hoot of laughter from Jack and the teamsters shamed away his wrath. They were all sweet on the greenhorn Missouri girl. They admitted they were fond, too, of Sunset Liz and her playmates, but they were in a different class.

"Liz has throwed in with me," Jack said, speaking low so that Huffenberger wouldn't hear him. "I can tell you she ain't packin' much flour in them barrels in her wagon. Course they are writ out as flour on the bill of ladin' she showed to the army at Cantonment Sparks. That's why she has to wait until dark to refill her jug with pain killer. Two of them barrels is nigh brimful of pain killer that'll sell high in Montany."

"So Liz knew she was headin' for Montana?"

"Shore. She's an old timer. Take a big chance for that Montany gold money. Same with Dot and Dollie. Why them Montany miners'll pay a dollar a dance up there in any hurdy gurdy dance house."

So Jane Payne was the only innocent lawbreaker in the train. Even her guardian had winked at the breach of army regulations in the hope of making a big gain in Montana.

Sam's anger was stirred at thought of the risk to which the girl and her property had been put but he could not raise any loud objections to the plans of Jack and old Barberry. He had been engaged in similar lawless activities all winter. He could warn Jane Payne if the train reached the river safely, that she must separate her wagons from Jack's guidance. There would not be much point now in explaining what a great risk she had taken unwittingly.

"You called Canady Pete today, hard," Sam said. "Told him he had double-crossed you."

"He did," Jack answered, adding cautiously, with a glance around the camp-fire circle and lowering of his voice: "He tipped it off to the army about this train headin' north. That's why we got stopped. It was all Pete's fault in the first place."

"How come?"

"He was supposed to have stuff on the train headin' for Montany. He got tied up on some other trade. Was away from his post when we pulled out. He thought I had turned him down." Jack raised his cup and spoke in a whisper as he held the cups to his lips. "But while I was ridin' outside circle this afternoon, I found the shoulder bone of a buffalo. Pete had left it for me. You know how messages are writ out here on the trail on buff'ler bones. He had writ fer me to meet him about first dark around the mule herd. Got a new deal to talk over."

Sam tensed up. But he kept his voice calm as he asked Jack, "How'll you find him?"

"We've dealt before. He'll signal where he is. Three owl hoots. Keep it up until I locate him. Them soldiers on guard will never figure anything from the hootin' of an owl. That's why Injuns and hombres like us use owl talk for signallin'."

Red Dog broke up the talk with a loud demand that Sam sing a verse from his buffalo song. Sam didn't feel like singing tonight. He had determined that he would overhear the pow wow between Jack and Canada Pete if he could outwit his guard.

He could look down the line of fires and see the women of the train eating their suppers. Jane was laughing merrily as she sat on a blanket at the side of

Lieutenant Prime, plying knife and fork on a tin plate.

Prime joined in with his pleasant baritone laughter. It all irritated Sam. He had saved her hair from the Sioux but now she wouldn't throw him a pleasant word or a smile. Seemed like she had taken offense because he had called her a corn-fed from Missouri. He had meant it merely as a compliment. And then she had caught him drinking from Sunset Liz's bottle of pain killer.

"Well here she goes, boys," Sam drawled, and throwing back his shaggy hair he cocked his eye at the first star to twinkle in the evening sky.

Oh take me back to the buff'ler days,
When Injuns whooped in the prairie haze,
Deadwood gals show you a high old time,
But Missoury corn-feds wasn't wuth a dime.

That verse checked the mingled laughter of Jane and Lieutenant Prime. But it brought the corporal of the guard on the angry gallop to Red Dog's fire. The corporal tonight was Spike Dillon. He was riding a tough brown Indian pony, and carrying his Springfield across his saddle fork.

"Pipe down on that fool singin'," he told Sam angrily. "You want to bring the Injuns down on us?"

"Nothin' wrong with my singin'," Sam answered sullenly. "Red Dog and these other hombres don't object. Of course, some other greenhorns might be too danged nice to like it."

"Special orders for the night now goin' into effect is first for you to shut up," Spike yelled out. He nodded to Huffenberger, who had jumped up and come to attention. "See that he keeps his bazoo shut from now on."

"Yes sir," answered Huffenberger.

"Don't call me sir," snapped Spike. "You only call that to an officer."

Sam stood up, grinning. "A corporal in the infantry," he drawled to Huffenberger, " is about the lowest form of life there is. Don't waste no politeness on him at all."

"You shut up, Sling," Spike snapped. "Little more chin music from you and we'll gag and hog-tie you."

Chicago Jack, Red Dog, and the other teamsters were listening with wide grins to Sam and Spike. They were also enjoying the discomfiture of Huffenberger, still at strict attention, and vastly puzzled as to just how to address Dillon with respect.

"You might call his sweetheart," Red Dog suggested.

"Or darling," said another.

"What's a dog robber?" asked Jack. "Ain't that some kind of a corp'ril?"

But Dillon glared down at them with cold anger. "Don't forget you're all prisoners. The army is issuin' orders tonight in the hopes of savin' this train from the Sioux. What we're up against is not a laughin' matter. If there's any gent or gents want to buck the army further—" he ran his eyes over the circle of bearded men around the fire. "We can show 'em quick how wrong they are."

Chicago Jack stood up and stretched his arms. "Aw, Corp'ril," he drawled. "We didn't mean anything. Just a little joshin' to make us forget the danged war whoops." He glanced up at the darkening sky. "We'll be hookin' up in another hour," he went on. "I reckon I'll get in a little sleep until then."

But as he strolled off, Sam knew that Jack wished to get away from the corporal so that the latter could not interfere with his intended meeting with Canada Pete out by the grazing mule herd.

Sam was putting his own mind to ways and means to listening in on that pow wow. Spike Dillon would be a difficult man to outwit tonight. But poor old Huffenberger, although he always meant well, was a big green recruit. So Sam dragged a blanket from the wagon and announced that he would roll up under the vehicle for a little sleep.

"He's tricky," Dillon cautioned Huffenberger, "keep your eyes peeled."

"Shucks," Sam complained, crawling under the wagon, "where would I escape to tonight? With that Kickin' Horse and his war whoops prowlin' the ridges."

"You're one man," Spike answered tartly, "we don't take any chances on."

Sam rolled up in the coarse blanket so that not even his toes or the tip of his black head was in sight. Red Dog, glancing under the wagon as he fed sagebrush to the flickering fire, told Sam he would sweat himself to death like a sick Indian in a medicine wickiup. But Sam only grunted and humped up under the blanket like a couple of sacks of flour.

The supper fires had been built outside the wagon corral so that men could keep an eye on the chain guard of soldiers, and the herd of grazing mules. There was always the fear that the Indians might attempt to stampede the herd.

Huffenberger sat down with his back to one of the huge rear wheels of the wagon where he could keep an eye on Sam beneath the vehicle and listen to the teamsters talking around their fire. Dusk began to fall swiftly for the sun had long since disappeared. A chill little breeze began to blow from the north.

"That Sam Sling wasn't so loco when he rolled up that way," said Red Dog. "I reckon I'll get out my buff'ler coat."

"This danged country," growled another teamster. "Only two seasons. Winter and July."

The fireside circle broke up. Teamsters strolled off toward their wagons for the short rest before the mules were brought in for the night march. Sam heard the small noises of the camp die away. Shadows were deepening across the range. Spike Dillon rode past on another round of his guards and Huffenberger sprang to his brogans with a clatter of belt and rifle.

Sam seized that moment to work his way out from under the blanket. He humped it up as though his body still reposed under its folds. He lay in the black shadow cast by the rear wheel opposite Huffenberger. Listening intently, he heard Spike caution the guard and Huffenberger's reply that the prisoner was fast asleep. When the corporal had ridden on around the train, Huffenberger resumed his seat with his back to the wheel near the fire, and his feet stretched out to get its warmth on his toes.

Sam felt a pang of remorse at his escape which might put poor Huffenberger in the guard-house when the train reached the river. But as he squirmed away from the wagon, circling his way down the inside line of the train, he told himself that he would return if he succeeded in overhearing the talk between Jack and Pete. He felt almost convinced that it was Pete who had betrayed the trappers to the Sioux since Chicago Jack had charged the trader with betraying the wagon train to the army.

The crawling mountain man only encountered one moment of danger before he slid under a wagon down the line and snaked his way toward the mule herd. He almost bumped head on into Sunset Liz as she emerged from the rear of her wagon carrying a bottle. Although Sam was moving on silent moccasins, she sensed his approach, and turned with an exclamation of alarm.

"Hist," he whispered harshly. "It's only me. Sam Sling."

She confronted him, tightly gripping the black bottle.

"What are you after?" she asked. "Another drink of pain killer."

Sam grinned. "You said you always filled up after dark."

"It ain't dark yet."

"I'll wait then. Don't let the danged army know you seen me." And he slipped off into the shadows.

Out in the tall sagebrush that grew between the train and the mule herd, he lay flat on his stomach, listening for the measured hoot of an owl. The first darkness had covered the earth. Behind him, the line of fires had been built up brightly in response to Prime's order. Then came the signal intended to guide Chicago Jack to the meeting with Canada Pete.

Sam followed the direction of the call. He grinned in the darkness, edging his silent way past a sentry whose thudding boots could be heard for a hundred yards. If Indians were not fearful of the darkness, he thought, they could slip easily past any soldier guard, however vigilant.

He lay waiting until the owl hoot reached his ears for the second time. Pete was growing impatient, waiting for Jack. If Jack didn't hurry, the mules would be bought in, and hooked up for the night march.

The third call from Canada Pete led Sam to the rim of a small ravine where Pete was crouched.

CHAPTER 14

Sam's first impulse was to take Pete by the throat and force from him a confession. Since his arrest by the army as a trespaser, it had lain heavily upon Sam's mind that in saving Jane Payne from the Sioux he had unwillingly betrayed his two partners. Tom Bear Mouth and Shorty had vowed not to rest until they had avenged the murdered Buffalo Hump and his missing wife, the Night Star.

But Canada Pete was not a sentry with untrained ears like Private Huffenberger. Pete would not be taken easily. At the first alarm he'd slip away in the darkness toward the pony which he had undoubtedly hidden outside the camp before arranging this rendezvous with Chicago Jack.

Sam restrained his burning desire to achieve something that might square his account with Bear Mouth and Shorty. He lay in the shadows above the coulee, silent as a dead man, until he heard a rustle of movement in the brush, and the low challenge from Canada Pete. The answer of Chicago Jack came in a harsh whisper.

Sam cursed himself for not attempting to crawl nearer the two frontiersmen. But he dared not run the risk. He lay straining his ears but hearing nothing except a low rumble of talk. Chicago Jack spoke out once or twice in an angry, argumentative tone but Pete cooled him off with his usual line of soothing whining talk.

Just what deal the two had struck, Sam could not ascertain. He heard only one sentence from Pete that changed his plan for the night. Just before Jack began his stealthy retreat to the train, Pete said, "I can't tell for sure until I get to Paint Rock Sinks. The chief's there."

"You're double-crossin' again."

"No. You're safe until I can go and come from Paint Rock."

Chicago Jack growled. "I guess I got to trust you."

In the darkness, the two parted. Sam lay deep in thought. He could find his way, even by night, to Paint Rock Sinks. It was far off the beaten trail in an eroded desert country that lay around twenty miles north of the river. It had gained its name from deposits of colored minerals in the rocks from which Indians manufactured their paint. There would be a moon tonight but Sam didn't intend to attempt the trailing of Canada Pete to the Medicine Paint rocks.

Capturing the range-wise trader by night would be difficult. But if he could secure a mount, Sam thought he might scout out Paint Rock Sinks before dawn came. If Kicking Horse had established his main camp there, such a venture appeared so dangerous that Sam dared not consider all the risks involved. He felt that he owed it to Tom and Shorty to risk his life in the attempt. He might see or hear something that would lead to revenge for Buffalo Hump and the Night Star. There was also the remote chance that he might gain some knowledge that would benefit the wagon train.

Huffenberger would wind up in the guard-house. The army wouldn't bear down too hard on a raw recruit for allowing a prisoner to escape. Of course, Spike Dillon, corporal of the guard, would also come in for punishment. But Sam shrugged off the thought of Spike. Let Spike lose his chevrons. He'd learn not to turn on an old-time bunky so harshly.

Sam was working his way out to the grazing mule herd in the hope of gaining a mount somehow. Of course, he'd be forced to make a bareback ride. His waist belt and the trailing lariat of the mule he caught must suffice as a crude sort of bridle. He wasn't certain as to just what a mule would do once he attempted to capture and ride the beast. The entire guard might turn out shooting.

Luckless Spike Dillon, making another round of the guards before the herd was driven in, solved the problem for Sam. The corporal rode past Sam who was hiding behind a sagebrush. Fifty yards ahead, a sentry challenged sharply, "Who's there?"

Spike sang out, "Corporal of the guard!"

The sentry had heard the thud of hoofs. Complying with strict army regulations, he issued his order.

"Dismount! Advance to be recognized."

Infantry guards never permitted a horseman to ride down upon them.

Spike checked his pony and slid from the saddle. He tied a rein to the top of a nearby bush and began walking slowly toward the waiting sentry.

Here was Sam's chance to gain a mount, all saddled and bridled and at the expense of Spike Dillon. He had to wait until Spike had reached the sentry. In the poor light, then, if Spike sighted him mounting up, he'd be too far off to recognize Sam. Sam's impulsive nature had overcome the caution which Tom Bear Mouth and Shorty had attempted to instill. He wanted to get away from the army, head south, scout out the camp of Kicking Horse in Paint Rock Sinks. He could not wait for Spike to reach the sentry. He slid silently out from his covering sagebrush and approached Spike's pony.

As he untied the bridle rein, the Indian pony flung back its head with a snort of alarm. Ten yards away, Spike Dillon whirled, flinging up his Springfield.

Sam jerked the pony around to protect himself from Spike's bullet as he got into the saddle. The pony was stubborn, a hard-headed, iron-mouthed brute. Sam gasped out an angry curse. "Stand hitched, you danged keg-head!"

"Sling!" Spike Dillon roared, cooking his rifle. "Sling! You're under arrest!"

Sam got a toe in swinging stirrup. The pony was uneasy because he was being mounted from the left or white man's side. He had forgotten, in his hurry, that this was an Indian digger, and that Indians always mounted from the right side.

Dillon wouldn't fire without another challenge. He was lunging toward Sam as the latter struggled into the McClellan saddle.

"Sling!" Spike cried again. "Is that you, Sling? Get off my horse!"

Spike wasn't certain that it was Sam. He had guessed only by the sound of Sam's voice as Sam cursed the pony.

Now Sam had gained the saddle. He kicked the pony in the ribs.

The sentry, awaiting his corporal, heard the drum of hoofs as the pony broke into a gallop. He was puzzled at the sound, but true to orders, he roared out an alarm.

"Turn out the guard!" he bellowed. "Post Number Three! Turn out the guard!"

Spike Dillon, dropping to one knee, fired on the man who had taken his horse.

Bent low in the saddle, kicking the pony to headlong speed, whipping him with the ends of his bridle reins,

Sam heard the whistle of Spike's first bullet passing over his head. He could also hear the loud confusion as the whole camp came to life. Herd guards were shouting in the gloom, bunching up the mules. The sentries of the chain guard strung around the wagons were bawling back and forth. From the post of the main guard in the rear of the train, Sam could hear a bugle call the men to arms.

He dared not ride directly toward the mules, not wishing to stampede them. He veered to his right to circle the herd and its attending guards.

The pony picked up a sagebrush stub with a forefoot and almost pitched over on its spotted nose. Half thrown from the saddle, Sam hung to the reins while the pony struggled wildly to regain its balance.

A mounted guard loomed in the night, coming on the gallop. Sam kicked his mount so mightily in the ribs that he believed he had fractured a heel.

"Halt!" the guard roared. "Halt!"

Sam dared not halt. He ducked his head and belted his pony on through the tall sagebrush with the ends of the reins. The guard's gun blazed as he passed on the run. The blasting explosion, the red muzzle flash in the darkness, put terror into the Indian heart of Sam's pony.

Sam crouched, hanging to the taut reins, letting the little animal work its stout legs like pistons. He heard to his rear, another blast from the guard's gun, then a beat of hoofs. The fool was chasing him. Sam swung around in his saddle.

"Wagh!" he yelped, like a wolf, giving a fair imitation of a Sioux war whoop. "Wagh!"

That dread yelp checked the guard where perhaps a white man's gun would not have succeeded. For all the guard knew, Indians might be attempting to jump the herd. He did not wish to be lured into the prairie shadows where they could pull him off his horse and take his scalp. The guard reined in.

Finally clear of the camp and its guns, Sam checked his mount. He turned off toward the southeast in the direction of Paint Rock Sinks. He dared not take any trail that a horse could travel easily in the night. He might encounter Canada Pete on his way to a rendezvous with Kicking Horse.

Sam did not fear that he would encounter hostile Indians. Only in emergencies, did the warriors roam around at night. That was the dread season when the ghosts walked. Warriors preferred to stay near their cheerful camp fires at night. There were some exceptions. Warriors of great courage sometimes stalked a rival band's camp to steal horses, and sometimes women.

Figuring that he had to cover at least thirty miles before he reached the Painted Rock country, Sam moved steadily on while darkness covered the earth. The wind carried a chilling bite for it had switched to the northwest and was blowing down from the snowfields of the distant Big Horns. The moon would not rise for a couple of hours. A drift of clouds obscured the stars in the black sky. It was a melancholy time for young Sam Sling. As his pony lurched along, feeling for secure footing in the darkness, all Sam's fears and worries flooded his heart. He could have turned the pony and made straight for the Platte River to join up with Tom and Shorty. He'd be safe. He knew that. They'd curse him for a coward and a man who could not be depended upon to keep a promise. But he'd save his life and his hair.

But if he made this dangerous ride and could scout out the Sioux camp, he might discover some clue to the fate of the Night Star. He hoped that he'd discover the nature of the bargain that Canada Pete had made with Chicago Jack.

He also knew, with certainty, that so far as the army was concerned, he was now truly an outlaw. He had stolen the mount of the corporal of the guard. A far more serious charge than trespassing in Indian territory. They'd shoot him on sight. As for Jane Payne, by this time the girl would know that he was a scoundrel. Prime would see to that.

She'd have more cause now to hate him than when she over-heard him remark that he liked corn-fed girls. She'd take the army's viewpoint that he was a white renegade who had stolen a horse to get back to his Indian friends. Sam shook his head gloomily as he rode along through the darkness. Shorty was right about women. A man should never get too deeply interested in them. Nice company on a big spree in town. But they broke a man completely down when he let his mind dwell too much upon their entrancing curves, their bright blue eyes, their shining hair. A sober man on the frontier, Sam thought, was a fool to think of anything but horses, pelts, wild game, and the ways of hostile Indians.

If it hadn't been for that fool girl, this minute he'd be safe on the river with Tom Bear Mouth and Rocky Mountain Shorty. They'd be laying out plans for the trailing of the war party that had jumped the beaver cache and stolen the Night Star. They'd be honing up their skinning knives for Indian hair.

Far off in the darkness he heard the melancholy call of what he believed was a rain crow. He'd never seen one of those birds. Always called before a storm came. And then, while he guided his pony through a patch of giant sagebrush that reached to his waist, he heard the hooting of an owl.

He reined instantly. He dared not dismount. He was barely breathing. It might be an owl. But he could not forget that the hooting of an owl was the signal favored by Canada Pete. And it was favored because it was also the customary call of prowling Indians.

He heard the hooting a second time. It seemed to be near at hand. A man could not tell much about an owl. They could throw out their hoots as coyotes did their howls. Best thing was to sit here like a block of wood and listen.

Sam could not forget that he didn't have a knife for his defense. Approaching the hostile Sioux camp, he had to depend upon his trained senses. If he missed one bet, some Sioux tepee would be adorned with a very thick scalp of black hair.

The owl hooted again. This time from some distant ridge. Sam heard the quavering howl of a coyote rise toward the stars. He felt little quivers of fear run up his backbone. He felt certain that a coyote wasn't howling. This was not courting season. In the summer, if the little gray wolves felt like singing, they generally waited until the moon came up. The moon had not risen.

Sam would have bet a stack of blue chips that it was some Indian buck over on that ridge answering the owl hoot signal with a coyote song. Perhaps they were passing Canada Pete through whatever scouting lines they had thrown out above the wagon train. Whatever, the reason, it behooved a lone white now to move with utmost caution if he expected to die at a green old age with his hair straight.

Sliding from his saddle, Sam moved around to where he could keep a tight hold on the bridle reins, and put a hand over the muzzle of his pony if the brute sensed another pony and tried to nicker a greeting.

The stolen mount stood at ease, his eyes half closed. The animal was undoubtedly dreaming of acres of knee-high bunch grass. It wasn't worrying about losing its hair, or the sorry reputation that might be held of it by buxom Missouri girls.

The hours of the night seemed to stretch out immeasurably as Sam waited tensely in the sagebrush draw. But the owl—if it had been an owl—apparently had flown away in search of prey. The coyote no longer wailed from the ridge. At last, Sam dared to move on. But for a time now, he stayed down in the draw, down where kindly shadows would hide him, where he could strike instantly for some hiding place if owls and coyotes became howling Sioux horsemen riding out of the night.

Though he had felt the icy cold sweat of fear, he had made up his mind with certainty. He would scout out the camp of the Kicking Horse. He owed that to his partners. If he died, he would go down fighting to the best of his unarmed ability but secure that he had died while trying to remain true to the frontier code of never breaking a promise given to a partner.

CHAPTER 15

The moon rose above the dark hills, a pale and watery moon half shrouded by a drifting rack of clouds. But it offered a better light for the trail. The owls and the coyotes were silent. Sam mounted the brown pony and took to the high ridges, knowing he had to make better time if he hoped to arrive at Paint Rock Sinks before Canada Pete concluded his pow wow with the Kicking Horse.

Knowing the Sinks, Sam decided that any camp would be near the only spring of good fresh water within many miles. He was passing now through a low country which had eroded away through the centuries under the continual punishment of sun and wind and frost. Soft earth had been washed down the draws. Only spectral shapes of hard bare rock remained, spires queerly shaped like the towers of ruined prehistoric cities, vague clumsy towers of rock that resembled coiled serpents and horned beasts.

If the sun had been shining, its rays would have revealed the raw slashes of color in the broken walls that Sam was passing. Mineral of red and green and black could be easily dug out and pounded up with animal fat to form the body paint of Indians.

The red bands came here often to stage their feasts

and dances, to secure the paint for the war path and the scalp trail. It was a haunt known to all tribes of the northwest, a site sacred to the medicine chiefs, seldom fought over by rival bands since battles here might anger the Wakan Tanka, the mysterious ruler of the heavens.

Crossing a plateau littered with broken rock, a distant thudding like far off thunder reached Sam's ears. He halted his horse and sat listening for a moment. He heard the distant beat of a tom tom. The council was in progress. Canada Pete had reached the Sinks, and was holding his pow wow with Kicking Horse.

Sam picketed the unsaddled pony before he made another move toward the camp. He wrapped his lanky back in the saddle blanket. If he should encounter some Indian boy night guarding the pony herd, he could muffle his head in the blanket and pass himself off as an Indian.

But it was more likely that since this band was on the war path, the braves would not be burdened with more than their favorite war ponies. And these prized horses would be picketed out wherever their masters built their wickiups.

Sam ran the chance that Indian dogs might be with the band. It was the invariable custom of Indian dogs to bark at any white man who came near. But warriors seldom took dogs with them on a raid.

The greatest risk Sam ran, as he crept toward a rimrock which overlooked the big spring in Paint Rock Sink, was that he would encounter some Indian stationed as a guard to prevent any invasion of the council.

Muffled in his blue cavalry saddle blanket, Sam crawled to the rim. He lay flat on his stomach gazing down upon a scene of barbaric splendor. A blaze of light from the dancing flames of a huge fire at first dazzled him. The loud insistent beat of the huge war drum, the shrill cries of the painted singers who sat around it, boomed against his ears. He could hear the shrill piping of the tiny medicine whistles fashioned from the wing bones of birds with which dancers were carrying on some sort of ceremonial dance. He heard the rattling of the medicine drums, and the deep-toned chorus of warriors seated around the council fire, singing to the boom of the drums and the dancer's whistles.

Sam found himself looking down upon a band of at least one hundred warriors. He counted a half dozen naked braves squatting around the huge tom tom fashioned from the fleshed skin of a buffalo and a hollowed cottonwood log. A pole had been erected near the fire. From the top fluttered a black mat of long hair. A dozen warriors, naked except for paint and beaded breech cloths, were stamping around this pole, blowing their medicine whistles, flourishing knives and stone-headed war mauls.

This was the scalp dance with which the braves of the band were quickening their courage before nerving themselves for the main battle with the white soldiers in the fort, the akicita owanka. The soldier camp.

A half moon of grim warriors sat around the fire and the pole, watching the dancers. They were not in full paint. Some wore blankets pulled up over their heads. There were others gaudily streaked in red and black with eagle feathers in their coarse black hair.

The dancing and the music ended abruptly. The scalp dancers retired to the grim and silent crowd. A man stood up and walked out toward the pole. He wore a red Hudson Bay blanket. He let it drop to his shoulders. Sam saw that he was an old man with long white hair. He was waving an eagle plume fan as he began to harangue the council.

Sam caught enough of the Sioux words, the graceful

hand signs, to understand that opinions were divided in this band. Kicking Horse desired a big war. But this old man with the eagle fan—which marked him as a chief—was bidding the young men to stay off the war path. They were brave but the pony soldiers were many. They had wagon guns that were loud as thunder, and could blow up a man and a horse a long ways off. If the Kicking Horse had a claim against the white man, let him go to the Indian agent and seek justice. Why send out runners to call on the Ogallalas, the Uncapapas, the Minneconju? Why draw warriors of these tribes into a war—a kicizapi—in which they would gain nothing but quick death.

Let these young men remember the time not so many winters back, when just a few soldiers in the mountains above the hated fort on Piney Creek, had broken the might of Red Cloud. The Sioux had thought the pony soldiers would be armed with guns that had to be muzzle loaded. So they had allowed the whites to fire, then had rushed them, expecting they would take scalps before the akicita could reload. But the walkaheaps—the infantry—had a new sort of gun which could be loaded swiftly from the rear end. They had reloaded so swiftly that they had caught the charging Sioux by surprise. They had cut them down as a boy slashes ripe fruit off a choke-cherry tree with a lashing quirt. That had been a sad and bloody day for Red Cloud.

When the old man ended his talk, and covered his head with the end of his blanket, the Indians in the ring who were not in paint, uttered deep agreement. They had nothing to gain in a big war. Kicking Horse could not show them where they would gain anything at all. Better to remember the pipe of peace they had smoked at Fort Laramie in 1868 when they made their marks on the white men's talking paper.

A tall Indian in full paint strode to the center of the ring. He was magnificent, a good six feet tall in his moccasins, hawk-faced. Upon his bare chest was painted the outline of a bucking pony. Around his upper right leg was knotted a bandage.

Sam knew that he was looking down upon Kicking Horse, the war chief who desired a big war with the soldiers down in the fort on the Platte. Here stood the leader of the scouting party that had jumped the beaver cache camp. That scalp, dangling from the top of the pole, was the hair of Sam's faithful Shoshone friend, the Buffalo Hump.

The war drum boomed. The painted scalp dancers sprang forward. Warriors leaped up from the council ring, flashing their weapons, saluting their war chief. A medicine man, wearing the shaggy scalp of a buffalo, still adorned with the polished black horns, led the frenzied scalp dance.

Sam gritted his teeth, clenched his hands as he saw that the medicine chief wore the blue blouse of a soldier, a blouse with the white chevrons of an infantry sergeant upon the sleeves. And slanted around the medicine man's waist by a cord was a brass army bugle.

Here was the big medicine, the wakan of Kicking Horse. The coat and the horn he had taken away from the akicita. It had gained him a victory in the mountains. He had taken the hair of a brave chief of the Snakes—the Shoshones.

The Kicking Horse raised his right hand. The tom tom pounding ended abruptly. The dancers and the shouting warriors resumed their seats. Kicking Horse refuted the calm arguments of the old chief who did not desire a big war. The Washingtons had lied again to the Sioux. They had said they would not allow the long hairs to overrun the buffalo country along the Powder

River. But they had broken their word as they had before. The long hairs were like the swarms of grasshoppers that ate up the good buffalo grass. They would starve out the Indians. Now was the time to drive them east of the Big Muddy river. Let those of the Ogallalas and Uncapapas who did not wish to fight, go to their camps and live like squaws.

"Waxte!" roared the warriors who were hot for war. "Good!"

But the Kicking Horse would not depend upon words alone. He would show the big medicine he had lately acquired which would bring the Sioux a victory over the white akicita. He reached out his right hand and a warrior handed over a rawhide sheath. From it the Kicking Horse slowly drew a rifle. There was at first not a sound around the council fire. Savage eyes were centered on the shining gun, the mazakan.

The war chief raised it to his right shoulder. He slanted the barrel toward the heart of the fire. Then he began to race the lever. He flashed six roaring shots, ripping tearing bullets that flung blazing embers around the council circle. Then he held the gun high over his head, a savage grin on his gaunt paint streaked face.

"Wakan!" he shouted. "Mazakan wakan!" The magic gun of the long hairs, the gun that could shoot as fast as a warrior could race the lever. He would see that the fighting Sioux acquired plenty of these guns if they would fight. Armed with such weapons, they could laugh in the faces of walkaheaps armed with rifles that had to be reloaded after each shot.

"Waxte!" roared the warriors. "Good! Good!"

Sam saw that now many of those who had not yet painted for war had tossed aside their blankets. They could not withstand the temptation of securing a magazine rifle. They would give a pony load of buffalo robes for such a gun. A beaver pelt for each cartridge. They would even give up a favorite wife for such a weapon. The magic gun. The wakan mazakan.

A white man stepped from the shadows into the firelight. The dancing flames glistened on his shaggy black beard. There stood Canada Pete with folded arms while Kicking Horse explained that here was the good friend who would furnish the warriors with the fast shooting guns. A pony, laden with pelts, was led into the circle. This was the price that Pete had set on a gun.

But when Kicking Horse waited for agreement from Pete, the smiling trader shook his head slowly. The baffled warriors began to mutter angrily. But Pete spoke smoothly. He desired a gift of the prairie from the brave Sioux. He was a lonely man. He required a woman to tend his fire and cook his meat. Kicking Horse knew of such a woman. Let the Sioux provide the woman.

The chief looked down upon the squatty shaggy figure of the trader. But Canada Pete, knowing that he held high cards since presumably he possessed a secret stock of the guns from which had come the chief's weapon, waited with a smile on his lips. When the chief grunted that this had not been in the original bargain, this gift of a woman, Pete answered that he would return many women to Kicking Horse. There was, in fact, a beautiful white woman who would shine like the sun in the lodge of the great chief. She had hair that was the red color of the sun on a frosty morning. She was from a far off land called Meesouree.

Sam gasped. The renegade was offering Jane Payne to Kicking Horse. If he had held a rifle then, Sam would have put a bullet through Pete's black heart and died willingly in the fight that would surely have ensued. But he was powerless. He could only listen, sick at heart, as this grinning renegade sold out his own color for profit and the gift of woman flesh.

The bargain was struck. A pony load of furs for a gun. The big drum boomed. The barbaric dancers circled the pole on which dangled the scalp of a brave enemy, a chief of the Shoshones.

A figure wrapped in a blanket was led into the ring while Canada Pete stood waiting and grinning. Warriors streaked in red and black war paint whipped off the blanket while the medicine chief in the army coat attempted to blow his bugle.

There stood the comely Night Star, widow of Buffalo Hump. She was taller than most Indian women. Her figure was shapely, half revealed in the scanty wolf robe with which they had covered her limbs and dusky bosom. Brass wire bracelets flashed on her wrists. She wore anklets of wire around her slim ankles, and a necklace of white elk teeth around her graceful neck. Her blue black hair had been combed down smoothly and vermillion paint drawn along the center parting. There was red in her smooth round cheeks and her full red lips. She resembled a princess of the distant land from which these Indians were said to have come in ages past. The firelight gleamed softly on her glistening smooth brown flesh, her half exposed breasts, her long legs.

Sam's breath quickened as he looked upon the tempting splendor of the Night Star, this faithful woman who had resisted all amorous advances from white men in the winter camp, this squaw who had been true to her mate. Had she now gone over to the enemy?

He could not tell. She had lived enough around the whites to know how to tempt a trader like Canada Pete. To win her, Pete had betrayed the camp in the mountains and aided in the murder of her husband. She had been painted and adorned as the prize of Kicking Horse. But Pete had won his point. She would be given to him as the chief's gift on the prairie, the token that the gun deal with Pete was waxte—good.

They would attack and attack along the river until Pete had arranged to deliver the guns at the crossing on the stream of the Wolf. But they must not bother the wagons. The vehicles were required to haul the guns and ammunition. Once Pete had had the wagons lined up, but the raid in the mountains had come up, and the wagons had moved away. He laughed. But he had sent the whoa-haw soldiers to bring them back so he could use them to haul guns to the brave Sioux. He bent his head and put his right hand to his cheek, the sign for sleep. In three sleeps, he said, he would deliver the guns at Wolf Creek to the Sioux. For Kicking Horse he would bring a red-haired squaw to take the place in his tepee of the woman who had been given to Pete.

"Waxte!" the warriors shouted.

The drum boomed again as the Kicking Horse led the Night Star to Pete. The trader took her gleaming painted body in his arms. Around the embracing couple, a blanket was thrown. They stood there, mated in the savage way, beneath the dangling scalp of the woman's murdered husband.

Sam Sling turned and crawled back to where he had tied his pony. A winter's catch of beaver was not worth it. Never again would he carelessly flout the law, however arrogant he might deem it. He believed that Chicago Jack, a free-booter but a brave man, had thrown in with Canada Pete on the gun deal. And as he saddled his pony for the ride to the river, Sam was picturing also the painted half naked body of Jane Payne in the bloody arms of Kicking Horse.

CHAPTER 16

Sam Sling broke from the rough badlands hills above the broad Platte Valley when the sun was man high over the eastern divide. He figured that he was two hours behind usual riding time from the Paint Rock Sinks to the head of Wolf Creek. But the tough brown pony was tired and hungry. He had delayed, back on the trail, to water the horse and allow it to graze.

He told himself, as he checked for a look over the winding course of Wolf Creek, that he could do with a little breakfast himself. He grumbled at Spike Dillon because the latter had not tied a bag of emergency rations to his saddle. Sam had pulled his belt up to the last notch, what he termed a Spanish breakfast.

Since he had made the long lap of his ride during darkness, he had not encountered any roving Indians. But he forgot his hunger and became alert when he jogged out of the hills. Not far distant, he saw the Wolf Creek outpost from which Lieutenant Prime had drawn his command of mounted scouts.

Sam made a cautious circle around the location. He didn't wish to be jumped by some sentry, and then subjected to hours of cross examination by whoever was in command. Captain Budhouse, his former company commander, was ten miles on at Cantonment Sparks with almost a battalion of infantry, four lettered companies. Budhouse should be informed immediately that Kicking Horse had the guns.

Sam wasn't challenged at the outpost. Taking courage, he examined the desolate wind-beaten array of caves dug in a cutbank above Wolf Creek which had housed federal doughboys. All were now deserted. There were a half dozen of these holes in the wall. Blankets had been taken from the crude, home-made board bunks. Sam couldn't find so much as a can of bacon to take the edge off his appetite.

The brown pony fared better. A stack of wild hay had been shaped up a few yards away from the edge of a small log shack that had served as the headquarters of the outpost commander. The provender had been hauled from Sparks to feed the mules and ponies of the mounted scouts.

An attempt had been made to link the outpost with Cantonment Sparks telegraph line but this had been given up as a failure. Roving Indians burned down the poles. They cut the wire. Since telegraph wire had a special magical meaning to them, they considered it big medicine and shaped up bracelets and anklets for their squaws and themselves. Night Star had worn telegraph wire ornaments at the Paint Rock bridal ceremony with Canada Pete.

As Sam remounted and headed on toward the river, following the general course of Wolf Creek, he saw that some of the burned poles had been reset by repair patrols. As the charred ends had been chopped off, these poles were now near the surface of the earth. A man could stand in a saddle on a horse and reach the wire.

A quarter mile south of the outpost, he swung over the Wolf Creek crossing, and paused to examine the ground. This was the spot which Canada Pete had named as the place where he'd turn over the fast shooting load of rifles and ammunition to Kicking Horse. Above and below, the creek cut its way between rather steep banks, but here a shallow gravel ford offered good footing for men and horses. South of the crossing, the road ran into a short narrow canyon that pierced a low range of hills. When Sam jogged through the canyon, he wrinkled his nose at the odor of something dead on the air, and saw two big turkey buzzards circle away from a carcass in the grass not far off the main trail.

He didn't fancy examining the carcass on an empty stomach. But with Indians on the war path, he might find something of more serious import than a dead horse or game animal. He couldn't forget that his partners were abroad on this range. With the outpost deserted, there was always the chance that a traveller along the road would have his hair lifted by roving Sioux.

But Sam only lingered a moment over the buzzard's banquet. It was a dead pony, sprawled out and so long dead that the body had swollen and the upper legs stuck into the air. Sam wondered what form of death had overtaken the digger but he didn't pause to make any close inspection. Too many buzzards and blow flies. He rode on.

Toward noon he came out on the Oregon Trail winding along the north side of the Platte River. He was now inside the trespass line run by the army against whites intruding on Indian territory. On flats that were muddy during stormy seasons, he saw a width of ruts of wagon wheels a hundred yards wide where settlers had turned off the main course to escape bog holes. Sam saw the customary debris of the Oregon Trail, the empty bottles and barrels, old clothing, white bones of buffalo and work stock, rotting furniture cast off to lessen weight, a ragged dress once worn by a baby, fluttering in the wind from a gray old sagebrush.

There were other marks along the trail, cairns of stones not far from the road marking the graves of men, women and children who had not lived to reach the promised land. Sam shook his head and rode on. These greenhorns, he reflected, would risk most anything to lay hands on gold in Montana or California. Of course, some had headed west seeking new homes. The transcontinental railroad now ran westward through the southern end of the territory but plenty of covered wagons still stayed on the old trail, going as fast as a mule or an ox could walk from civilization to the Pacific.

Sam's jaws tightened grimly when he came down to the grassy elbow on the river where Canada Pete had established his trading post. Pete had erected a couple of good-sized log shacks of cottonwood cut from the nearby river. Around the buildings were arrayed round pole corrals, a big stack of wild hay, several dugouts, even a boarded up shack in which Pete stored ice that he cut on the river in the winter. Pete had been here before the army established Cantonment Sparks, a mile east on the trail. He had a reputation as a sharp dealer but there had been no proof of wrongdoing against reds or whites.

Knowing that Pete had a cache of arms somewhere, Sam ran his glowering eyes over the post wondering where the guns and cartridges would be hidden. No time now to make a search. Anyway, Sam thought, let the army take that end of it.

Desiring to eat before he reached the cantonment, Sam tied up at the rack in front of Pete's main building. A four-horse outfit and two or three saddle ponies were also lined up along the rail. Sam's first glance at the riding stock was indifferent. Then his eyes narrowed. He moved over to one dust-caked Indian diggger. This was the pony Shorty had ridden to the top of the peak the last time Sam had seen him. No sign of the horse Tom Bear Mouth had ridden.

For a moment elation swelled Sam's heart that his old partner had saved his hair and reached the river. Then his spirits fell. A reckoning was due with his partners and he was never much of a man to mouth out excuses for neglect of duty.

The post door was wide open. Pete let it stay that way in summer time so that flies could not only enter but also drift out. A big round table near the greasy trading counter over which had passed a small fortune in buffalo robes and beaver pelts was ringed by several bearded men in trail rig. Sam saw a black jug on the table.

One man at the table reached for the jug as Sam entered. The rank odor of trade whiskey gurgling from the jug into a tin cup reached Sam's nose. It reminded him of the smell of Sunset Liz's painkiller. Beyond the table, he saw Pete's wife, a quiet Indian woman moving around the counter, waiting on trade in the absence of her mate. She was called Little Bird, although she was fat. She was of the Ogallala Sioux but she had been rightly married to Canada Pete by a black robe father several years before. This explained why Pete was regarded by the Sioux as safe to trade with.

Sam wasn't thinking about Little Bird. His eyes were on the man who was filling the tin cup. The man was Rocky Mountain Shorty. Shorty's garments were ragged and covered with trail dust. He looked as though he had just emerged from a sandstorm. He was mumbling to himself as he poured the whiskey. His hand shook so that he spilled whiskey all over the table.

Another bearded man yelled boozily, "Go keerful, ol' man, with rotgut you ain't buyin'."

They were all half drunk. He looked around for Tom Bear Mouth but the Shoshone wasn't in sight.

Old Shorty was ordinarily a merry man. But something today had soured him. When his drinking companion reproved him Shorty took offense. He staggered up from the chair, reached down and whipped his long skinning knife from its beaded belt sheath. He seized the man who had bought the whiskey by the end of his shaggy beard and jerked his head forward. Shorty's eyes were glaring and red-rimmed. He rasped out that he could cut the throat of any man there who deemed him a cheapskate. It wasn't his fault that circumstances had broken him. He'd bought plenty of drinking whiskey from Pete before this and they all knew it. Any more fool talk and he'd go to work with the skinnin' knife.

A man in a red shirt, across the table, unlimbered a six-shooter and lined on Shorty. "You drop that knife, you locoed old galoot," he wheezed, "or I'll drop you."

The man whose beard Shorty had seized sat in paralyzed fear, eyes popped out like a big bullfrog. He dard not move or breath.

Shorty was so drunk that he didn't fear the drawn gun. He shrugged his scrawny shoulders, and tickled the throat of the bearded man with the edge of his knife.

"I'll have my steel into Jake here," he growled, "before you can pull off your iron!" Then suddenly his anger faded and sorrow overcame Shorty. Releasing the beard, he dropped into his chair. He shook his head and the tear rolled down from his rheumy eyes. He didn't put up his knife. "They've all quit me," he moaned. "Boys, yuh just can't blame for bein' soured on my likker. I had two good pards, but they both turned down ol' Shorty. Wimmen was their curse, boys. Wimmen!" The sobs shook poor old Shorty.

They forgot that he had just threatened to cut a friend's throat. They put up their guns, filled their cups, drank and wept consolingly with him. Even the man with the beard said that he would have cut out his tongue if had known Shorty would take his warning in an unfriendly way. In a moment Shorty had thrown his arm around Jake's shoulder and was sobbing.

Sam stepped over gingerly and touched the old mountaineer on the sleeve.

"Hey, old man," he said. "All your pards ain't quit you."

Shorty quit sobbing. His body tensed. For a long moment he said nothing. Then he came out of the chair as though a wasp had stung him. His eyes blazed with a mad red light. He poised the skinning knife for a thrust and slavered the foam of wild rage all over his dog dirty ragged beard.

"Pard!" Shorty squalled. "You're a hell of a pard! Turned me and Tom down for a female. We both seen it from the butte. Soft on a female! By Cracklin," Shorty dived for Sam in an effort to drive the skinning knife into his breast. Sam wouldn't have hit his drunken old friend for a fortune in gold. He backed up, and tripped over a box of sand placed on the floor for tobacco chewers to use as a spittoon. Shorty rushed upon him, eager as a weasel for hot fresh blood. Sam was fighting around to regain his feet. He warded off Shorty's wild knife slashes but the whizzing blade opened up his sleeve. He even felt the red bite of steel along his forearm.

It looked to Sam as though he'd be forced to knock out Shorty to save his own life. But Little Bird had been trained by her husband to handle tough customers. She came sidling around the end of the counter, moving swiftly for a woman who had picked up so much fat living the easy life of a trader's wife. She reached up and tapped Shorty on the back of his narrow head with a wooden mallet. Not a hard tap. An experienced snap in the right spot that took all the fight instantly out of Shorty. His eyes fell back. His legs came apart at the knees, and he folded up. She caught him expertly as he fell and lowered him to the floor. Sam bent and picked up the knife that had fallen from Shorty's hand. There was no fight in him. He hoped none of the men at the table would take up Shorty's quarrel.

None did. They were deep in liquor but they regarded him with cold eyes. There was no greater offense on the frontier than to turn down a partner. They wouldn't even fight him in fun. They just sat there in accusing silence, watching Sam Sling. He knew Jake, the man who had drawn the gun. They were mule skinners, men like Red Dog. They would give the shirts off their backs or their last bottle to a friend. They would share their last slice of bread with even a stranger. But any man who turned down a partner—his name was pizen.

"After he sleeps it off," Sam said to Little Bird, "I'll talk to him. I'm ridin' down to the cantonment. I'll be back for supper."

"Old man feel heap bad!" murmured Little Bird. She was a woman who had once been as pretty as Night Star. Not for anything would Sam have told her that her husband was unfaithful. Little Bird had always dealt fairly with the partners. She shook her neat black head. "He lose track of Bear Mouth. You no come either. He come in here yesterday. He heap broke. One pony. Say pony soldiers, Injuns get pelts. No money even for buy fire-water. Heap bad."

She was dragging Shorty around the counter as Sam pulled out for the cantonment. Jake and the rest had resumed their singing and drinking. Life was like that along the old Oregon Trail. Here today and gone tomorrow.

The battalion of infantry was in tents along the river. Sam passed the picket lines and corrals where mules and ponies were cared for. He saw the slow moving boys of the stable guard shoveling hay and manure around under the direction of a sarcastic sergeant. He recalled when old Bootle had ridden herd on him as he did that duty. Two big stacks of hay stood near the round corral where mules and horses could be broken. Then came a log shack at the head of a long street of dingy wall tents. A brisk sentry in blue walked post in front of the building. The flag fluttered gently from the top of a pole in front.

This was cantonment headquarters. The sentry was a stranger to Sam. He gave his dirty buckskins, his greasy shock of black hair a wry glance but he passed him into the shack. There was an outer office in which sat a fresh-faced young lieutenant back of a desk marked "Adjutant."

Sam gave his name and announced that he had an important message for the cantonment commander. A door led to an inner room but the partition was of thin planking. This door was suddenly flung open. Framed there stood a stocky bald-headed man in a rusty blue uniform and with a shaggy tobacco-stained brindle mustache framing his hard thin mouth. It was Captain Budhouse.

"Sling," snapped the captain. "You got the nerve of a river gambler to come here." He turned to the adjutant. "Lieutenant," he ordered crisply. "Call in the guard. Put this man in the guardhouse!"

CHAPTER 17

Sam was carrying Shorty's skinning knife on his belt. At the captain's angry order, his own temper flared for a moment. He dropped his hand to the knife haft, stepping toward the commander as he did so. Then his wrath faded. A man risked his hair to find out something of value to the army. After he starved out on a hard ride to fetch it in, they threw him in the mill for his trouble. No use trying to fight the whole army. All he wished to do was tell old Budhouse about Kicking Horse.

Budhouse misinterpreted Sam's instinctive reach for the knife as a hostile move. As did the young adjutant. The lieutenant came flying around the end of the desk, struggling with clumsy fingers to unsnap a pistol from his belt, bawling all the while for the guard. The Captain backed into his office, warning Sam at every step to drop the knife and submit to arrest.

The adjutant freed his pistol and rammed the barrel against the small of Sam's back just as the sentry came plunging into the office with bayonetted rifle thrust forward for a quick jab.

"Aw fer God's sake," Sam said disgustedly, "put up your guns!" If I'd aimed to kill Cap'tin Bug—Budhouse, my steel woulda been in his neck afore he could spit. All I come here was to tell you the Sioux are shapin' up for a war. They got a chief called Kickin' Horse. He's all fired up to hit the river most any time."

Budhouse frowned and nodded to the adjutant. "Take away his knife. Then have the guard stand by here in the outer office."

Sam passed over the knife. He'd buy another at the trading post from Little Bird. Then he remembered that he was flat broke if Shorty had lost the spring take of pelts. The Indian woman hated to give credit to mountain rovers but she liked Sam and he thought she'd probably stake him to the knife and the few other possibles he lacked. Then he'd sober up Shorty. They'd hit the trail and attempt to find Tom Bear Mouth. And then maybe Tom would wish to head out for his sister and Canada Pete.

Closing the door on the adjutant and the sentry, Budhouse sat down at his desk. Sam stood across from him, dead tired on his feet. This old man had been a cpatain for ten years, grown gray in the starved out service, drawing a captain's pay now for handling a major's job. He was like Rick Sling who belonged, heart and soul, to the army. Budhouse always held a high regard for Rick, boosting him to sergeant over Bootle. Studying the stumpy, pot-bellied officer, Sam recalled that Budhouse had not signed charges when Bootle accused Sam of striking a non-commissioned officer. But Budhouse had scornfully curled up a thin lip when Sam took his discharge after one enlistment.

"Well," Budhouse said curtly. "What's all this about Kicking Horse?"

Sam told him. He included his belief that Canada Pete intended to deliver rifles and shells to the Sioux at Wolf Creek crossing within three days. Sam left out the part about the Night Star. That would only lead to complications about bringing in the illegal beaver hunt. Sam still labored under the impression that once he had convinced the captain of his good intentions, he would be freed.

Budhouse jotted down a few notes while Sam talked. He unrolled and scanned a map of the country, his pencil pointing to various places mentioned by Sam. Then he leaned back in his chair, scratching his stubby mustache with one end of his pencil, and said, "Well, after all this, I reckon you think the army ought to pin a medal on you."

"Hell," said Sam, "I didn't set out to be no fool hero. Thought you should know about the Injuns."

"You spoke of being with that wagon train but didn't have much to say of just how you happened to get there. The army's curious to know where you were about ten days back. If you'll give me a good fair answer to that, maybe I'll take more stock in your yarn about these war dancing Sioux."

Sam frowned. If he told the truth, he must reveal that ten days ago he had been on treaty territory, happily trapping beaver with Shorty and Tom Bear Mouth, unaware that savage plans were afoot to rob and kill. If he talked up now, he'd involve his partners. He already had enough to explain to Shorty and Tom without dragging the blamed army into the story too.

Budhouse sighed. "Ten days ago, the paymaster started from this post to pay off the half company stationed at the Wolf Creek outpost. Those men—like the companies here—hadn't been paid for five months. Corporal Bootle drove the ambulance. A young bugler, who had been here on sick leave, rode in the seat with the corporal. The sergeant commanding the outpost, who had been here on some business about rations, rode ahead on his pony to scout out the road. Another mounted guard trailed the ambulance."

The captain paused and gazed out the dirty window before resuming. "There was about five thousand dollars in gold coin in the chest inside the ambulance. We presumed the armed escort was heavy enough to see it through. We were wrong. A gang—some of them in paint and feathers like Indians—jumped the outfit in a little canyon this side of Wolf Creek."

Sam nodded. That was where he had seen the dead pony.

"They stampeded the mule team and upset the ambulance. They killed the paymaster, the young bugler, and the rear guard."

"What about the sergeant?"

"Corporal Bootle got into the brush. He said later the last he saw of the sergeant he was galloping away from the scene as fast as his horse could gallop."

"Goin' for help to the outpost," Sam said, "or—"

"Or saving his own hide. That's what Corporal Bootle said."

"I seen a dead horse in that canyon today. Dead some time. Reckon it belonged to one of the dead men, rear guard or sergeant. Carcass was used up some by buzzards. Wasn't a roan though."

"The sergeant isn't dead. He was riding that roan. He came into the outpost on foot. He swore that they had hit the pony in the neck with an arrow. The animal bolted. He was forced to shoot it to stop it. Bootle swears the sergeant is a liar."

"Bootle never could drive mules," Sam said, pondering. "Reckon that's why the army always had him doin' it. Like with the wagon train—"

The captain cut him short. "Forget Bootle. The gang—white men or Indian—they got the five thousand in gold. One of them left forty dollars gold to pay for a military funeral for the lieutenant paymaster."

"How about the enlisted men, the bugler and the rear guard?"

"They knew the army would bury them free of charge." The captain added. "They took the bugle young Jones was carrying. And they also stole the blouse off the back of the sergeant's saddle after he had killed his pony."

Sam's eyes glinted. He leaned on the desk. "It's my guess, captain, that Kicking Horse and Canada Pete was in on the holdup. At that Paint Rock shindig, the Injuns sported a bugle and an army blouse as strong medicine."

"Indians," the captain said curtly, "aren't much interested in gold money."

Sam knew this for a fact. Money meant little to wild Indians. Being savages they took more stock in goods they could see. They seldom took money for their pelts from traders. They were paid off directly in blankets, guns, paint and beads and the like. Knowing nothing about money values, they were cheated most of the time but happily didn't know it.

The captain didn't lay the blame for the raid on Indians. He intimated that white renegades, disguised as Indians, had robbed the paymaster.

"Canada Pete," Sam cried. "He organized that raid. Then, later, he traded the pony soldier coat and bugle to the Sioux, makin' 'em believe it was heap strong medicine. Captain, you round up this Canada Pete and you'll have the he-dog of all this hell that's started to pop."

"Pete has been a good friend to the army. Often assisted us with valuable information."

Sam growled. He had also succeeded in pulling the wool over army eyes. It was not unusual on the frontier where wily interpreters had played Indians against whites before this. Chicago Jack had accused Pete of tipping off the army to the route of the wagon train. He had also accused Pete of being a double-crosser. Sam scratched his black hair. He didn't believe Jack would sell rifles to Indians but Jack wouldn't hesitate to rob the army. Nor kill any soldiers who might be in the way. That way of providing stolen money for an officer's burial would be Jack's idea of a rich joke.

Sam was all ready to blurt out his accusation of Chicago Jack when Captain Budhouse interrupted. "Now you're the young Sling who goes in for Indian clothing and ways. You quit the army for that. I'll bet you've worn moccasins so long you toe in when you walk. And if they put army brogans on your feet again, you'd develop broken arches from the high heels."

"Now listen, captain."

Budhouse pushed back his chair. He stood up. "After the robbery, I put out orders to arrest all suspicious characters who could pass as Indians and couldn't tell a good story of where they were ten days ago."

Now Sam understood why Spike and the rest had scorned him. They were under orders not to talk about the murder and robbery. Even Bootle hadn't talked. Finding him in suspicious territory, garbed like an Indian it's likely the soldiers had decided that he was one of the gang. Since Sam wouldn't tell where he had come from, vague suspicion had grown into a certainty.

There was the point that the doughboys hadn't been paid off for five months. Stealing pay, in their eyes, would be a worse crime than killing the paymaster. To be robbed by a former army man, that would be a good cause for hanging.

Sam shrugged and nodded. Now he was all fixed up. The army hated him as a payroll robbery suspect. Shorty and Tom believed he had quit them for a female. The female believed he had flirted around with Sunset Liz and the girls.

"If that's all, captain, I reckon I'll be goin'."

The captain nodded. "Go right ahead."

Sam turned, repressing the old soldier instinct to salute the captain. He opened the door and stepped out into the adjutant's office.

He stopped. His jaw gaped. His eyes popped.

Three belted soldiers of the guard stood waiting for him with fixed bayonets. The corporal in command was his old friend, Jimmy Kerry.

"Confine him," the smooth-faced adjutant ordered.

Kerry regarded Sam with stony face. "Will you come peaceful," he asked, "or shall we put you in irons?"

Sam stared back at his former comrade's harsh face and accusing eyes. His whole world had now turned upside down. All because of a few beaver pelts which he had believed, against good advice, could be lifted from under the noses of Sioux and army alike. But Sam was now past showing anger or even pleading his cause. He dropped back to the sardonic humor with which a mountain man sees his way through a spell of tough luck.

"How do you feed in the mill?" he drawled.

"You ought to know. You spent enough time in it."

"Hash, I hope. I could stand a hell's slew of hash. Let's go."

They marched him from the shack, past the tent which housed the guard, and into another flimsy shack which served as the guard-house. An armed sentry unlocked the door. They thrust Sam inside and slammed the door on him. He heard the key grate in the lock. The light was dim since only one small window had been cut in the wall. It was high up, and barred. There were large cracks in the walls through which some light slanted for green whip-sawed lumber always warped out here on the plains.

"Shucks," Sam said. "Who wants to get out? They'll be blowin' mess call in another hour."

He saw three men seated on the double-tiered bunks across the room. Coming in from the sun, he couldn't at first recognize them. Assuming they were fellow prisoners, penned up for minor breaches of discipline, he approached them. He called out cheerfully, "Well, boys, how does old Cap'tin Budhouse feed? Sow bosom and tack as usual."

Then he halted. The grin froze on his hairy face. He knew these prisoners: Spike Dillon, Private Huffenberger. And—his own brother, Rick Sling.

They stayed seated in silence, watching him with eyes that looked as level and dangerous as the aimed barrels of cocked rifles.

CHAPTER 18

Huffenberger swung his big feet from an upper bunk and dropped to the dirt floor. Red with anger, he advanced on Sam with fists coming up.

"All I ask," sputtered Huffenberger, "is one good punch at that grinnin' mush of your'n."

Spike Dillon, seated on the edge of the lower bunk beneath the private, dodged his head as Huffenberger descended. Then he jumped up and walked toward Sam, his dark face twisted with anger. "I'm the oldest soldier here," he said coldly to Huffenberger. "I rate the first punch at him."

Sam slowly backed up. Of course he knew why they were here. Prime would have had only one recourse after Sam's escape. To put the corporal and the private under arrest for allowing it. It was odd that they had reached the cantonment before he did.

All that broke up the immediate fight was the interference of Rick Sling. He stepped between the two enraged soldiers and Sam. He looked his brother over bleakly but didn't extend his hand.

"You still seem to have your old time ability of getting into trouble. Haven't seen you since your discharge four years ago. And when I do, danged if it isn't in jail."

"It's a poor place for a family reunion, I'll admit," Sam answered, "but you seem to be in the same place yourself. Last I heard of you, you were sporting a sergeant's chevrons and headed for top when old McNeal retired. Now you're in the hole with me."

Spike attempted to push past Rick Sling but the sergeant thrust him aside. Rick was a bulky man, with iron gray hair and a smooth face browned the color of an old saddle. When he laid his big paw against Dillon's chest, he moved him out of the way as easily as a grizzly bear knocking over a bee-hive. Huffenberger, still angry, tried to go around Rick's other flank but Rick didn't waste a hand on him. He merely blasted a harsh order. "Get back to your bunk."

Huffenberger looked offended but retreated as commanded.

"I suppose you know why they confined you?" Rick asked.

"Near as I can make out I happened to be about fifty miles north of Wolf Creek when a jag of army pay was lifted and some soldiers killed. Since I dress like an Indian—like about nine tenths of the civilian inhabitants of this territory—the army figures maybe I helped out on the deal. Cap'tin Bughouse—"

"Call him by his right name," growled Rick.

"I call things as I see'em, Rick. I'm not in the army now. I make a ride to let the army know Kickin' Horse and the Sioux are painted for war. So they slam me in the mill."

Spike Dillon cut in, speaking between his teeth. "The captain forgot to say that you'll be charged with horse stealing. Government property. My horse. Soon as I can sign the charge that I identified you as the thief. You know how a guilty horse thief rates in this territory even among civilians. You'll be lucky if you make the pen.

They might take you away from the army and hang you."

Sam shook his head. There was no answer to Spike's charge. He had stolen a pony. Of course, he hadn't stolen it for personal profit. He believed he was doing the army a service. Perhaps he should've consulted with Lieutenant Prime. But he felt that Prime wouldn't have understood. He could but have peached on Chicago Jack for the deal with Pete. Jack could have denied it. It would have been one man's word against another's. It appeared to Sam at the time, and even now, that the theft of the pony had been forced upon him. But he didn't care much. He had brought the warning of Indians and a renegade's deal in guns to the captain. He had been jailed for his pains. His brother had greeted him as though he were a skunk.

Then and there, Sam determined that as soon as they had served up the night mess, he'd start figuring how to break out of the guard-house.

"Well," Rick interrupted his thoughts. "Talk up. What about this pony stealing and why in the world come in when you knew you'd be arrested?"

"It's a danged long story," said Sam. "When do we eat?"

"You don't eat," growled Spike. "Not with us."

"Forget this kid stuff," Rick said impatiently. "The guard'll stop any fightin' in here."

"I still say this buzzard don't eat with us," Spike insisted stubbornly. "You ain't issuin' orders no more, Rick. You've lost your chevrons."

"I'm confined," Rick grated. "But I'm not busted. A good man gave me those chevrons. It'll take good men to take 'em away."

"A general court-martial," sneered Spike. "Cowardice."

Rick swung around. He swung a punch for Dillon's chin but Spike dodged. In so doing, he came within range of Sam's right fist. A red blur of anger had gone over Sam when he heard his brother termed a coward. Anger which he had sworn earlier to restrain around the dumb army johns. But calling old Rick a coward was too much. Sam swung from belt level, clicking his haymaker off Spike's jaw. Spike sagged at the knees. He wasn't knocked out but he sat helplessly on the floor, gasping for air. Sam's quick rage faded as quickly as it had arisen.

"I ain't particular who or what I eat with," he announced, blowing on his knuckles. "But I'll tell the world that I eat when mess call goes if I have to take this mill apart."

Rick shrugged and walked back to his bunk. "Thanks for steppin' in," he said, over his shoulder. "Of course, Dillon wasn't lookin' at you when you hit him."

Sam let that pass. He saw a stool on the far side of the room and went over and sat on it. Spike got up and staggered groggily to his bunk rubbing his jaw. Huffenberger sat on the top one, dangling his feet, and growling deep in his throat. Rick rolled a smoke and watched his younger brother in a sort of cold remote silence.

Mess was called and soon after a can of stew, hard tack, and a big pot of black coffee was brought to the prisoners. Corporal Kerry came in with the soldier who carried the provisions. He issued eating gear, for confined men weren't allowed to keep such things in the guard-house. They might dig out with a spoon or stab a sentry with a general issue knife or fork.

Sam ate until he felt puffed up as buffalo bloated on green greasewood. He stretched out his long legs and fumbled around in his possibles pouch for his old black pipe and the tiny black hunk of twist tobacco that he had hidden from Shorty when smoking ran low in the hills. He filled up the pipe. stepped over and lit it at the lantern which Kerry had placed on the center table, then resumed his seat. With his mind somewhat at ease since he had been fed, he emptied his possibles pouch hunting for something that might aid him in a break-out. The guard had taken away all dangerous articles such as Shorty's knife and a block of sulphur matches. But they hadn't lifted the arrowhead which Shorty had taken out of Sam's side.

Sam looked at the gracefully fashioned barbed flint head. A portion of the shaft was fastened to it. Sam recalled Shorty's remark that the shaft marks might provide Tom with a clue to the identity of the warrior who had used it. Warriors often put marks on arrows to prove ownership. That way they could claim credit for killed wild game or men.

Sam's wound had healed pretty well since the extraction of the arrow. In the pure high air of the west, infection seldom resulted if wounds were cleaned up within a reasonable time.

Rick laid his eating tools on the table and stepped over. He asked Sam where he had picked up the arrowhead. Sam gave him a vague answer. A Sioux had taken a shot at him. He had kept the broken off head and shaft hoping by the marks to prove ownership.

"So they put marks on them?" Rick asked. "I had heard of that." He held out a broken shaft end to his brother. "You know Injun stuff pretty good. Take a look at this." Rick handed him an arrowhead.

The marks were rather obscured by dried blood but Sam washed some of it off with cold coffee. He said finally that he'd bet the same warrior had once owned both arrows. He knew that his arrow had been fired by an Indian with the band of Kicking Horse.

"Then," Rick said, "it was that bunch of reds that jumped the paymaster. I don't know how much the captain told you about that deal but you've probably guessed by now that I was the sergeant whose pony was stampeded. Bootle claims I ran away."

Sam hadn't known when they put him in jail but he had suspected when Spike spoke of a charge of cowardice. The meeting with Rick had not been an affectionate one but Sam would fight any man in the world who called old Rick a coward. He got up and said as much. He also added that this was another example of army dumbness.

"Bootle's the one making the charge," Rick said grimly. "It's the captain who is standin' up for me. He'll probably be forced by army regulations to prefer charges on Bootle's say so, but he'll go to bat for me before the court. I'm dependin' on his help." He took another look at the arrow portions. "This may help out my case when I show 'em to the captain and he hears your story."

Sam gulped. Budhouse would want to know where the Indians had taken the shot at him. That would bring in Shorty and Tom Bear Mouth. Sam was a simple man. This trail was getting too blurred. Hard for a man to know which fork to follow. Couldn't let old Rick down on any help he required to clear his record. But he couldn't get the army tagging after Shorty and Tom.

Spike jeered, "Best thing you Slings can do is tell where you hid our pay."

Sam started across the room, hot to take on Spike. Spike, just as willing, jumped up to meet him. Huffenberger slid down eagerly to get in on the fight. But Rick Sling again intervened. This time he held off his younger brother. It was now Sam who yearned to wipe the nasty grin off Spike's swollen face.

"There's some truth to what Dillon says," Rick said wearily. "Fightin' won't help. It's up to us Slings to produce the gold to prove to these iron-headed soldiers we didn't steal their pay money."

"Us?" asked Sam.

"Sure."

Describing his part in the payroll robbery, Rick told Sam he had been riding ahead of the ambulance when he heard the yells and gunfire of the attack. He attempted to turn back but an arrow, striking his roan pony in the neck, stung the little horse to madness. It stampeded, running out of control. Drawing his pistol, Rick shot it to check its wild flight. Thrown off, stunned, he crawled into cover. Three painted raiders, galloping past the dead horse, halted. One dismounted and took his blouse off the saddle.

"When it was all over," Rick went on, "I staggered back to the wrecked ambulance. Bootle had taken to the brush. Only man left alive. He accused me of runnin' away. We started on foot for the outpost. I cut off the arrowhead shaft thinkin' it might be evidence. When I got to the outpost I sent word to the captain. He relieved me of command. When Bootle accused me of bein' a coward, he confined me."

But with the arrest of Sam, suspicion had been strengthened that perhaps the Slings had actually been involved in the raid. When Sam stole a horse to escape, Prime believed it so important that he sent a detail of scouts riding through the night to the cantonment with this new information for the commander. Spike and Huffenberger were sent in with the detail as prisoners for neglect of duty.

"The whole deal revolves around Canady Pete," Sam said, with a certainty he couldn't prove at this moment. "He's mixed up in all this hell. He's played a smooth game until now with all of us, trappers and army alike. But he gave himself away when I spotted him dickerin' with Kickin' Horse and the Sioux."

"Trouble with that is," said Rick, "that nobody but you saw all this dickerin' around. You'll have to tell the captain how you come to be prowlin' around in Injun country when the soldiers caught you."

"They didn't catch me exactly. If it hadn't been for that fool of a Bootle—" He frowned and shook his head. "Bootle hates you, Rick. You're in his way. He wants your stripes. I'd like to hang around and talk some with the cap'tin. He'd better hold an early pow wow with me."

"Why?"

"Because I'm going to get out of here and catch old Canady Pete red handed—somehow."

CHAPTER 19

Sam stayed overnight as a guest of the army. When it came to making some sort of break, he discovered that he could not turn his back on his brother. Rick disapproved of Sam's free-and-easy outlook on life. Sam, just as heartily, scorned his brother's loyalty to iron rules of army discipline. So Sam stayed around anyway. The night passed, and it was well past noon of the next day when the Slings were marched, under guard, into the captain's office.

Jane Payne and her fat old guardian, Barberry and Lieutenant Prime were waiting. More surprising was the presence of Canada Pete.

"You renegade," Sam growled.

Captain Budhouse interrupted sharply. "Sit down, Sling. And keep your mouth shut until you're asked to say something. I'm conducting a sort of inquiry here into some serious charges that have come up. One for instance against you, charging you with escaping arrest and stealing a government owned horse to get away on. So sit down!"

Sam sat down on a stool near the door. He didn't answer the captain. He kept his glowering gaze on Canada Pete. The trader sat at ease, vastly unconcerned.

Prime soon supplied the reason for the trader's return

to army favor. Pete had caught up with the wagon train after the first forced night march, shown a shortcut to the lieutenant by which ten miles of distance had been cut off on the hard drag to the river. The various owners and their outfits were now safely camped near Pete's post. The army was deeply in debt to Pete for his assistance.

"So far as your charge goes of this man having a store of rifles and shells on hand for sale to hostile Indians," Captain Budhouse said to Sam, "I'll add that a detail searched his property yesterday. No such articles were discovered."

Sam listened then drawled, "Can I talk now?"

"If you have anything to say."

"You never rated me high as a soldier, cap'tin. But in four years of service under you, I was never accused of bein' a liar. You're callin' me a liar now. I don't know where he cached his rifles and such, but he'll get 'em to Kicking Horse somehow."

The captain frowned, looking from Sam to the smiling trader. He rubbed his stubby mustache with his pencil point. "A man might change after he leaves the service," he said slowly. "Other things have come up lately such as the raid on the paymaster's outfit. Both you Slings are poor men. You'd be in a position to stage a mock Indian attack to throw off suspicion. Five thousand dollars in gold is a lot of money to poor men. A clever yarn to divert suspicion to some other man might be part of your plan."

Sam made no answer. His temper was rising and he knew that if he talked, he'd have the captain calling out the guard. The interruption of the captain's missing speculations came from an unexpected source, Miss Jane Payne of Missouri. She snapped to her feet, thrust out her dimpled but firm chin and said to Budhouse.

"It is amazing how ridiculous men can be. Just because you arrest a man fifty miles north of your silly trespass line, you accuse him of robbery and murder."

"We haven't accused him of that. So far it is just horse stealing. We'll charge him officially with that when Corporal Dillon signs the affidavit that he recognized Sling as the thief who took his pony."

"Don't put me off, captain. I heard most of the story about these Sling brothers when our train came in this morning. All the teamsters were talking about it. Said the army was about to accuse one of its trusted sergeants with cowardice because his horse got stampeded by Indians and ran away with him." Her eyes flashed. "When I heard the name of the man who accused him of cowardice, I knew it was a lie."

"The man who laid the charge was Corporal Bootle. He was driving the mules on the raided ambulance," Budhouse rapped out. His eyes narrowed. "I'd prefer, Miss Payne, that you confine your talk to actual evidence. We are not dealing with sentiment just now."

Sne sniffed. "Sentiment, shucks. Bootle knows very well that mules and horses frighten easily in an Indian attack. I also know it because I was riding with Bootle a few days ago when just such a thing happened. I came here today to tell you that if it hadn't been for Sam Sling, the Indians would have my hair, and also that of your lying corporal." She shrugged, turning toward the door. Sam was listening to her with a proud grin on his face.

Jane flushed and tossed her head. She laid a hand on the door knob but Prime sprang forward to open the door for her. She turned back to the captain with the scornful remark that no cold-blooded bandit in his right senses would have jumped into a fight with Indians to save a strange girl and a soldier. It was unthinkable.

"He saved you, Miss Payne," growled the captain. "Naturally you are moved by kindly sentiments toward him."

She flashed Sam a glance as she stepped like a queen through the door. "I entertain no kindly sentiment," she allowed, "toward a man who thinks I'm a Missouri cornfed."

She went out into the adjutant's office, escorted by the attentive lieutenant. The captain sat scratching his whiskers with his pencil. Canada Pete sat grinning. Sam Sling sat slumped in his chair with jaw hanging on his chest.

But Jane got no further than the outer office. The sentry backed in, seeking to disengage himself from a banged up old man who clung to his neck like a tree sloth. It was Rocky Mountain Shorty and he was insisting loudly that he be allowed to talk to the captain.

"Take your hands off'n me, you old drunk," raged the sentry. "I tell you the captain's busy."

The adjutant pushed into quiet Shorty but the mountaineer, releasing his hold with one hand on the sentry's neck, reached out and pulled the adjutant's nose. "All you brass buttons can't keep me quiet!" he snarled. "I ain't drunk none. I'm a free-born 'murican citizen, and gotter right to see any danged officer I want to. Taxpayer too, by Cracklin!" He pulled the nose of the adjutant a second time.

Budhouse stormed from his office followed by the Slings, Canada Pete, and the girl's fat guardian.

"Take that drunk down and throw him in the guardhouse!" the captain thundered. He turned on the sentry and the adjutant. "What do you mean, allowing this commotion around headquarters?"

The angry sentry tried to apologize. The adjutant couldn't speak because he had just released himself from Shorty and was feeling with both hands for his tweaked nose.

"Captain Budhouse," Sam broke in worriedly, "he don't mean nuthin'. Just on a spree."

Shorty wheeled around and took a flying punch at Sam. "Budhouse!" he bawled. "Call him by his right name. Bughouse! Old Bughouse. They're all Bughouse. All these whippersnappers and honest citizens south of the Platte. Makin' pets of the danged Sioux. All Bughouse!"

Prime assisted the sentry to quiet Shorty. Sam fired up and stepped in to help Shorty. A scrimmage ensued. Budhouse bawling for the corporal of the guard. Sam landed an uppercut on Prime's chin but the lieutenant returned a counter punch over the heart that put a dent in Sam's wind. Sergeant Rick Sling jumped in to help the captain, the two lieutenants and the sentry. Shorty, forgetting his soft-toed moccasins, kicked Rick in the shins and howled with pain when he hurt his big toes.

Jane Payne seemed anxious to get into the action. Canada Pete, never interfering, lounged in the office doorway, picking his teeth with a match, more interested in the girl than in the fight.

The guard came on the run. Shorty and the two Slings were hustled back to the guard-house. Rick looked aggrieved. The captain apparently hadn't noted that he had jumped into the fight to assist the army. Neither found an opportunity to reveal the arrowhead and portions of marked shafts to the captain.

Shorty was searched before being thrust into the mill. The corporal of the guard discovered nothing more dangerous than a half filled bottle of trade whiskey.

Once the door had been locked, Sam turned stormily on his old partner. "Now you've shore played the fool. Gettin' throwed in jail about time I got ready to break out and join up with you and Tom." He advanced on his old partner who was stomping a variety of the Indian corn dance in the middle of the room, and chanting like an Indian.

"Hi yah yah yah! Hi yah yah yah!"

"Quit corn dancin' you old drunkard! You smell like a distillery! Quit it I say."

When Sam took Shorty's arm, intending to help the old fellow over to a bunk where he could sleep it off, Shorty flung his arms around his neck and broke into tears. He laid his head on Sam's shoulder, sobbing that the danged army had done wrong to his young pard. The disgusted soldiers looked on and listened. Spike said bitterly that a man could get a cheap jag on just by breathing the air in here. Huffenberger asked Rick if he should manhandle the drunken trapper. Rick stood rolling a smoke, taking it all in with shrewd eyes.

Between sobs, Shorty whispered into Sam's ear. "Help me play out the hand! Tom's back. We'll beat the army yet."

Then Shorty's strength seemed to fade. He limped in Sam's arms. Sam picked up the scrawny old frame clad in dingy buckskins and toted it to the nearest empty bunk. He bent over Shorty, straightened out his legs and shaped a pillow for his head. Shorty's eyes were wide open, entirely sober. He was whispering so faintly that Sam could barely hear him. They had often whispered on the hunting trail when within sight of wary game or Indians.

"At dusk," Shorty cautioned. "Red Dog and Jake and the boys'll make believe they're a bunch of Indians attackin' the post. That'll attract the attention of the guard. Then Tom'll fasten one end of a long string of mule trace chains to the bars in the window. One good pull by four mules druv by Red Dog and we'll pull out the hull back wall of this jail."

Rick stepped up as Shorty quit talking. "What's he saying to you?" Rick asked.

"Aw, just drunken gibberish!"

Rick eyed Shorty suspiciously. "It ain't often these wise old owls jump an army captain in his office. Seems danged queer to me."

"Well," snapped Sam, "why don't you call in a couple of your army friends and tell them about it. They've all been so willing to help you."

"Now listen, Sam."

"Aw, shut up. This old man's my pard. He's worth more drunk to this territory than a half dozen of your Bughouses. Go on away and let him sleep."

Shorty was snoring and gurgling in his sleep. Huffenberger looked down from his bunk, complaining loudly to Spike Dillon that a man couldn't get any sleep with the old bum snoring. Spike, listening to the talk between the Sling brothers, called back to Huffenberger that a recruit had no right to sleep in the daytime.

"But here I am in the mill," Huffenberger pointed out indignantly, "with nothing else to do. I wanted to put in time whippin' that trapper, Sling, for gettin' away from me. But you ranked me out of that. When I try to sleep, another drunk of a trapper keeps me awake. I joined the army to soldier. Got a clean service record up to now. If I could get out of here, I'd go over the hill."

"You rave on like a guard-house lawyer," Spike growled. "If you did get out and went over the hill, where would you desert to? Reg'lar baby in the woods in this country." But Spike was only listening to the complaining rookie with one ear. He was more intent on trying to overhear the Sling brothers.

Rick had drawn Sam over near the door. Sam hadn't been able to quiet his brother's suspicions about Shorty's spree.

"You've got some deal ribbed up," Rick insisted. "He was whisperin' to you. I just picked up the last few words. Somethin' about pullin' out the back wall of this place."

Sam laughed and looked around the room. "Now how in the world would we do that? Sentry walkin' post outside this door. Post of the main guard next to us on the line. Only one window and that high up. Bars in it to boot."

"A man could drag one of these double decker bunks over and stand on the top one to reach the window. If he had some sort of tool—hack saws or somethin'—he could then cut out the bars so he could squeeze through the window." Rick turned with sudden decision to Dillon. "Come on, corporal," he commanded. "Shorty's got somethin' on him to break out with."

"The guard already searched him," Sam cried. "All they got was a bottle of rotgut."

"We'll search him again," said Rick. "You two hombres aren't leaving here tonight."

Rick started for Shorty's bunk. But Sam seized his brother by the shoulders. He swung him around and stared into his set face. "You mean that you'd try to keep us from makin' a break."

"Sure," snapped Rick.

"But Bootle's accused you of bein' a coward. You're in this mill tonight. And old Bughouse talked about us bein' involved in that pay robbery. Yet if you had the chance for a bust out, you wouldn't take it." Sam reddened with anger. He shook his brother savagely. "Dang you and your blamed army. Dumb until you die.

Why a court martial might find you guilty. You know what they can do to a soldier who runs away from the enemy."

"Yes. They can sentence him to be shot." Rick answered.

"You'd stay and take your chances!"

"I put in the best part of my life with the infantry, Sam. What I got, the army gave me. It ain't much. But until now, I've been respected by some damn good men. And one of 'em—this one you call Bughouse—he put a sergeant's chevrons on me. They haven't taken 'em away yet. They can't do that until a court finds me guilty."

"So you're stayin'? Trustin' in your luck. Prayin' Bughouse'll help you."

"Not prayin'. Stayin' because I am innocent. Stayin' because I respect myself. Stayin', too, because if I did go over the hill tonight, they'd be dang sure that I was guilty as hell from start to finish." Rick jerked away from Sam's clutch and walked over to Shorty's bunk. He grabbed the old man by the moccasins and snapped to Dillon. "Help me search him, corporal."

Spike snarled, never moving. "I'm not taking orders from you. Not while we're both under arrest."

Rick gave a heave that jerked Shorty from the bunk and flung him to the floor. Then he turned on the corporal. He ripped out army language that made Huffenberger's eyes pop. He wound up by rasping, "I'm still a sergeant. I'm pullin' my rank on you, corporal. But if you don't help, I'll do more than that. I'll break your neck with my bare hands." He waited a moment, hands planted on his hips.

Spike stood up slowly. He was a corporal. Rick was the sergeant. He growled sullenly, "All right. What do I do?"

CHAPTER 20

While Rick pulled rank on Spike, Shorty sat up rubbing his back where old bones had been jarred by hitting the hard-packed dirt floor. He still maintained a pretense of being drunk until Rick said sharply, "Stow that, you old bum! I've handled too many drunk soldiers in twenty years service to be taken in by you." He eyed Dillon. "You and Huffenberger stand off Sam while I take this faker apart."

Sam watched Dillon swallow his anger and take orders. He was surprised when Huffenberger, another of the soldiers who had lost their pay and been convinced that Rick had taken part in the raid, slid from his bunk and stepped to Dillon's side.

There was something, after all, to being a soldier. There were a lot of dumb things about the old army, the way they did things backwards, starved out and missed their pay. But when it came down to it they stood together. They respected one another above personal hatred and envy and greed. The Bootles were exceptions.

Dillon was long in the service, Huffenberger young. But they swallowed their anger and stood shoulder to shoulder at Rick's command.

Sam possessed nothing to fight with but his fists and

the stool against the wall. He bent and picked it up. He gripped it by one leg and he poised it, shoulder high. Now there was a grim smile on his lips and a light in his eye. He stood with his legs widely braced, and his black hair falling to his buckskin covered shoulders in wild disarray. He stood there, and he sang a verse he had just thought of between his teeth.

Oh take me back to them buff'ler days
When Injuns whooped in the prairie haze,
Army threw me in the can
But Sling will scrap for the rights of man.

When Shorty heard the song he bounced up to his moccasins and made ready to help his young partner. He put up his fists and wagged his beard, daring Rick to lay a hand on him.

"By Cracklin'," Shorty said shrilly. Army ain't busted you. But I shore will."

Rick paid no more heed than if Shorty were a buzzing horse-fly. He had twisted around to keep his eyes on his tall brother who was advancing, step by step, singing his weird buffalo song, and swinging the stool.

Huffenberger breathed hard through his big nose. "Sarge," he said. "He's apt to brain me with that stool. We can call for the guard."

Rick laughed. "Huff," he drawled. "You won't get hurt if he hits you on the head. But watch out for your feet. Remember what Stonewall Jackson said about the infantry. Take care of the feet."

Then Rick stepped out to meet Sam. He didn't put his hands. "Right pretty song," he said. "Now if you've showed how dang brave you are, you'll put down that stool and quit foolin' around."

Sam cut off his song. His hot eyes were hard on the

determined face of his brother. "You can give orders to Spike," he grunted, "but me and Shorty aren't in the army."

"You go out of here tonight and the army'll hunt you two down like mad dogs if it takes a regiment of infantry. There's serious things against us, Sam. We can't run away. We got to stay and fight for our rights." Rick smiled faintly. "The rights of man that you're always talkin' about. Once you ran away because you didn't like Bootle. I thought you had grown up, Sam. I'm surprised. You're aimin' to run away again from Bootle."

"They threw me in here without givin' me a show."

Spike Dillon cut in curtly. "You stole my horse. You got two soldiers throwed in here because you wanted to swing everything yourself." Spike stepped up beside Rick. "I've changed my mind a whole lot," he went on, "since I had time to think it over. I knew you in the old days, Sam. You were a fool like me. But I know old Sarge here too. He has wiped my nose off many a time when he could have had me slung in the mill for a six month's blind. I'm not figurin' now that either of you would mix up in killin' soldiers or takin' their hard-earned pay. But you stole my horse, Sam, and so—so you got to kill me first before you break out."

Rick said again. "Put down that stool, Sam. In the final windup, the army gives every man a break."

"Sky pilot talk," sneered Sam. But now he knew that he was talking loudly to choke down the queer impulses that were stirring his heart. Here was old Spike, admitting that he had been in the wrong about the robbery but angered because Sam had put a blot on his clean record. Here was that big dutch-faced recruit standing up to the guns although he feared that this wild looking mountaineer would cave in his skull for it. But what about Shorty? He had quit his partners once to save a girl.

Shorty had come here to help him even in the face of Sam's desertion in favor of a pretty woman. The trail forked. Which way would a man ride?

Old Shorty dropped his hands to his side. He had quieted down. He stepped out to the center of the room. He called to Sam in a weary way. "Sam, they hold the high cards on us. Put down the stool."

"I'll stay with you, Shorty, until the last dog is hung."

"I know that, son. But a danged passel of beaver ain't worth all this." Shorty stepped nearer to where he could talk to Rick. "We didn't like the danged army trespass rules. We don't like 'em yet. We figured it would be easy to lift a few prime pelts from the Sioux."

"I figured it, Shorty," Sam said bitterly, "and I've cussed myself ever since."

"We was all in it with you. Tom Bear Mouth, Buffalo Hump and the Night Star figured they had rights above army rules because they were Shoshones who had once trapped in that part of the Big Horns. Times had changed." Shorty wagged his head sadly. "Fellers like you and me must also change or pull out. The army comes here to set up civilized rules for folks that are different from us and the Injuns. Folks like those greenhorns you see in the wagon trains. Maybe their rules are the best now. We can see what happened when we busted 'em. A good man dead, his wife bad hurt, you and me in the army jug."

"Tom Bear Mouth's gone, Shorty. Maybe scalped."

"That's why I'm here. He slipped away while you was gone to scout the Sioux. He spied on a big pow wow in Paint Rock. He saw a war dance there. He wanted to find his sister and the Sioux who killed Buffalo Hump."

"Where's Tom now?" asked Sam, sensing something unsaid about the Shoshone's scouting of the Paint Rock pow wow.

"He couldn't stay for stray scalps, Sam. His sister got away toward dawn. From the wickiup of Canady Pete. Pete had felt so good he took too much of his own trade whiskey. Tom caught the Night Star as she was kneeling under the stars ready to bury a knife in her heart. He brought her in. She's a shamed thing, Sam. She won't talk or eat or anything. We got her cached out in the hills. Got to keep her away from knives."

"She acted like she had gone sweet on Pete," said Sam.

"He forced her. That's all, Sam. He wanted her so bad he framed that raid on the beaver camp. They got her before she could kill herself. They had jumped poor Buffalo Hump when he went down for water. She had no chance. The Sioux told her that Pete killed her husband. They wouldn't lay a hand on her for she was the wife of a brave man. But they wanted rifles so bad from Pete that he took a free hand with her. She thought, until the last, that she could get away and tell us. But she had no chance. She acted willin' at the pow wow because she wanted to get Pete drunk so's she could steal his knife and kill herself. She would have turned the trick if Tom hadn't found her."

The stark tragedy of the Indian woman's life turned the listeners cold. They could see that scene under the pitiless stars with the Night Star kneeling in the sagebrush, ready to drive her betrayer's knife into her broken heart. Then the silent approach of her brother who gave up any hope of instant revenge so that he could save his pitiful sister.

Shorty pushed aside his hunting shirt, revealing his ribby middle. His buckskin pants were held up by a rawhide belt. He laughed and unlooped it. When it was unwound, it reached out for at least ten feet.

"My weapon," he laughed. "The fool guard who searched me figured it was some sort of outlandish belt favored by us mountaineers. Of course, he never knew that I could slip it between the bars and lower it so Tom could tie the end of the trace chains to it. Then it could pull up the chain end and make a hitch on the window bars. After that, the fake Injun alarm to upset our guards while we made out getaway."

The guard-house had grown shadowy. The monotonous pacing of the sentry outside the door timed the recital of Shorty. The plan of escape framed by the trappers and mule skinners had been a wild one. But it might have succeeded. There were low hills in the rear of the camp covered with sagebrush. Four mules could be brought near the back of the building after dusk if the guard's attention could be turned in another direction by an apparent Indian attack. This building was flimsy, built of green, warped lumber.

"It might've worked," Rick Sling said, nodding wisely. He looked at Shorty with a kindlier eye. "You still smell like a distillery but maybe I've been wrong about you."

"Save it," said Shorty. "You and me live different lives. If we get out of this deal without bein' set by the danged army to make little rocks out'n big ones, we'll go our separate ways. Folks say there' still room west along the Rockies. Army ain't strong there yet. Time they get there," Shorty smiled faintly and touched his forelock, "some danged Ute or Nez Pierce'll likely have this hair."

"They'll have mine too," said Sam Sling. "Where you go, Shorty I side you."

"No, pard, " said Shorty. "Your brother's always been right about you. You've had your fling now. But you're young. The west is growin' up fast. Stay here and grow with it, Sam." He stuck out his horny hand. "Tonight, kid, we split the blankets."

"No!" cried Sam, half weeping. "No"

Shorty shook his head and grinned. "By Cracklin," he drawled. "While I was huggin' that guard in the cap'tin's office, I couldn't help seein' that pretty gal, Sam. She sure kept her eyes on you. She's the female you saved, Sam. Stay with her and grow up with the west." He winked. "And help increase the population. In a respectable way."

Soon the guard would enter with the lantern for it was near dusk.

"She don't like me," growled Sam. "I called her a cornfed. She don't like me."

"She is a cornfed. What's wrong about cornfeds? Tell her so, Sam, when the time is ripe. Takes a good buxom gal to beat this western country. None of your starve outs can do."

Suddenly, Shorty ended his soft talk. He turned his head toward the door. The pacing of the sentry could no longer be heard. Somewhere, far off, there was a dim sound like the splashing of water, then the faint rumble of drums rolling.

Sam and the soldiers, not gifted with the keen ears of the old mountaineer, now picked up the distant tumult.

"What is it?" Private Huffenberger whispered huskily. "Sarge—" he appealed to the veteran soldier. "What is it?"

Shorty spoke. "Ponies crossin' the river below camp. He laughed. "The boys ridin' in to make the guard think it's an Injun attack." He turned and gestured toward the bunk nearest the window. "About now me and Sam should be up there, lettin' the rawhide down to Tom for the end of his trace chain."

Sam said stoutly, still gripping his stool. "We can still make it, Shorty. We're partners."

"You're also my brother," Rick cut in. "Don't forget that."

"A man," Sam said, "has to pick his own trail where it forks. This old dog here," he nodded toward Shorty, "has stood up for me many times against the world. He's covered me up plenty when I played the fool. Maybe I'm playin' the fool now, Rick. But he has the call on me."

The sound in the dusk was increasing. The crackling of brush could be heard as though horses were being forced through the willows along the river.

"We are not goin' out Sam," Shorty said softly. "I meant what I said. We have split the blankets for keeps. I'm bad medicine for you, Sam, from here on out. What you need now is the Missoury cornfed to keep you on the straight and narrow—" he suddenly quieted.

The sound of a single shot cut the outside silence. Then a distant shout from the direction of the stables. "Post Number Four! Turn out the guard! Injuns!"

As though the alarm had unleashed all the hounds of hell, a wolf-like yelping choked off the sound of the shot and the sentry's yell.

"A good job for mule skinners," observed Spike Dillon.

"Gawd sakes!" cried Shorty. "That's the real thing. That's Sioux jumpin' us!"

Sam whirled and began to hammer on the door with the stool. Huffenberger fell to his knees and quavered that they'd die like rats here when the Indians reached the camp. Rick Sling turned and kicked him to his feet. "Stand up and be a soldier," he snapped. "Help pull over the bunks. We'll barricade the door."

Sam Sling groaned. "So much for the army," he said to Shorty. "Heavin' us in the mill. Nothing to fight with. To hell with your tall talk about peace and such. If I live to get out of here—"

Outside, the pounding of hoofs sounded loudly as horsemen swept through the lower edge of the camp. The war whoops rolled from painted throats. There was a ragged volley of rifle fire like corn popping in a skillet and the bawling of the sentry at the post of the guard. "Turn out the guard! Number One! Turn out the guard! Enemy in sight!"

His hoarse shout was silenced by the blaring of an army bugle. The musician of the guard had been booted out and set to blowing his instrument by some belted corporal. Sam recognized the thrilling notes of the call to arms. Along the line of tents, almost four companies of tough doughboys were turning out now, buckling up their cartridge belts, waiting even in the midst of clamoring death for the word of calm command.

"They got that sentry on Number Four," said Shorty. "But he got in his alarm first."

"How did you figure it as Sioux?" asked Sam.

"They're away down by the stables. We didn't figure to come that way. They'll set these soldiers a foot before the night's over."

Rick, assisted by Spike and Huffenberger, was pushing a set of bunks toward the door. He barked to the partners. "Come on and help."

"Give me a leg off that stool," said Shorty. "Maybe I can bust in one Sioux skull before they reach for my hair."

CHAPTER 21

The men in the guard-house knew they had reached the end of the rope. They had barricaded the door with the bunks but they understood this flimsy defense would yield quickly against the determined attack of maddened Sioux horsemen. They had armed themselves with the poor things that gave them an excuse to stand on their feet and die fighting. They had pried boards off the bunk, and held them now with the nails still sticking out. Sam and Shorty had divided the stool between them.

"Go on and sing," Shorty said to Sam. "By Cracklin', you always sung when we was in a fight. Go on and sing you buff'ler song, Sam."

Sam drew a deep breath. He began to sing softly because there was no use trying to pitch his voice above the roaring of the outside fight, the spitting rattle of rifles, the ringing whoops of the Sioux, the ever nearing beat of hoofs as the war ponies circled nearer to the guard-house.

Oh, take me back to the buff'ler days,
When Injuns whooped in the prairie haze,
The west was wild and men died hard,
But a man never quit on a good old pard!

"Thanks, kid," drawled Shorty. "Thanks." And he raised the hem of his leather shirt and blew his nose and wiped out his eyes. "Thanks! By Cracklin', a song to beat a war whoop!"

The door burst open. The noise of the fight poured in upon their ears like a flood torrent. Outside the dusk was bright with fire. The rattle of rifles, the hoarse shouts of command, reached their ears. The bugle had quit its braying.

Captain Budhouse stood framed in the doorway. He gripped a pistol. He was in his shirt. The Sioux had given the command no chance to turn out in fighting gear. They had cunningly staged their attack just before dusk when the soldiers were resting, waiting for the supper mess call.

Dusk also suited the Sioux. It was not dark. Spirits would not be abroad to bring misfortune upon the Sioux.

"Sergeant!" roared the captain. "Sergeant! Clear the door! Take those men with you! Arm yourself at the post of the guard!"

"Yes sir," said Rick.

"Make for the stables! Those hellions have fired the haystacks! They're trying to run off the mules and horses!"

Budhouse disappeared into the noise and smoke. He commanded four companies. Many in that command had never heard the war whoop of a hostile Sioux or the deadly whir of a war arrow past his ear. Many there, like Private Huffenberger, had never been shot over. Tonight they would become veteran soldiers of the infantry. Tonight, in the fury of fire and the shock of gunfire, they would know what it took to be a doughboy.

Not a man objected when Rick assumed command.

They thrust aside the bunks and went out the door on the run. The guard tent stood adjacent, between guardhouse and the headquarters shack. The men of the guard had been turned out and hurried down to posts along the river where brave men had died to sound the alarm.

A corporal was passing out Springfield rifles, and cartridge belts from which cased bayonets dangled. The corporal was Bootle. His hands were shaking and the sweat stood out on his fat face by the light of the smoky guard tent lantern. He choked out an objection when Rick and his grimy followers appeared.

Rick took him by the throat and flung him aside, then began jerking the long single-shot rifles from the rack, pitching them to eager hands.

"I feel better," sighed Private Huffenberger. His hands were shaking. He buckled up his belt, and clicked his brogan heels together, and stood waiting for orders.

"Fix your bayonets," rasped Rick. "Cold steel takes the heart out of most Injuns!"

Shorty, untrained in army weapons, fumbled with the long blade, cursing in a petulant way that he could do a better job with a skinning knife.

The line of tents stood on high ground above the river. The rear of the camp was dominated by a low ridge of sagebrush-covered hills. Three hundred yards from the right flank of the cantonment, the corrals and picket lines of the stables had been established. They were on lower ground, and nearer the river in order that stock could be watered more conveniently. Between the corrals and the tents ran the long road that men called the Oregon Trail.

Sam helped Shorty fix his bayonet. The tip of the deadly spike reached above the waspy little trapper's shaggy head. Shorty had looped the cartridge belt over his shoulder, bandolier fashion.

To the west and down below the guard tent, near the river brush, red flames flared up in the dusk. Black smoke rolled eastward in the teeth of a brisk wind from the mountains, hampering the soldiers who were fighting on the left flank of the camp. The Sioux had dismounted men, and sent these crafty warriors crawling up through the brush to set fire to the haystacks before they flung their mounted attack across the river. They had known the fire and the smoke would confuse and blind the pony soldiers and the walkaheaps.

"That was one time," Shorty drawled, "when the army and me agreed. When old Bughouse busted us out and told us to git guns."

The army, Sam thought, had thrown him in the jail. But in the pinch, it had also given him a chance to fight for his life like a man. He had to grin. After this was over, if he still lived, the army would send another detail to arrest him and throw him back in the mill. He could cover himself with glory in the fight tonight. But that wouldn't save him from the mill. The army never changed. Men changed but never the army.

"Dumb," Sam said softly, "but dogged."

He twisted his gaze about, using the eyes of an expert in Indian fighting. He believed this attack would be beaten off. The pow wow had decided, at Paint Rock, to alarm the cantonment garrison and pin it down, giving Canada Pete leeway for the delivery of his magazine rifles and ammunition to Kicking Horse.

This was the day of the second sleep. Anytime the next day, Canada Pete would make the meeting with Kicking Horse at the Wolf Creek crossing.

The Sioux had drawn back immediately to Sam's front. Doughboys had begun a slow advance toward the brush along the river. Now and then a Springfield boomed. There was also some sort of a fight going on at the far end of the line of tents but Sam didn't concern himself about that. Plenty of soldiers down there saving their hair and their packs.

Around the blazing haystacks, a continual clamor of battle arose from the stable. A few men were fighting to hold off warriors anxious to reach the ponies and mules.

"If the war whoops had magazine rifles," Sam said to Shorty, "by this time they'd have all the hair of those guards down there."

Rick flung himself from the guard tent. He was pushing Bootle ahead. Bootle's jaw waggled as he stuttered that he was on duty, charged with issuing out guns.

"Everything's passed out now," Rick said grimly. "You and me was together once on another raid. You didn't like the way I performed then. I want to give you a show now to prove how brave you are. Men are needed at the stables. Come along with us!"

The fire flared higher in the burning stacks. The light made clear the set faces of Rick's forlorn command. It outlined the scurrying forms of horsemen, darting from brush along the river, circling along the rim of the red light cast from the stables area.

"Take out in single file," Rick barked, his harsh voice ringing above the continual clamor of shrill war whoops, the bark of guns, the pounding of pony hoofs. "I'll take the lead with Sam and Shorty. Don't open fire until I pass the word. Light's bad. Target's out of good range."

He started off, Sam and Shorty close at his heels, the soldiers next in line. Sam was thinking, as he padded along, that most of the gunfire came from the army lines. This indicated to him that Canada Pete had not yet made a meet with Kicking Horse.

Rick, with an old soldier's skill, took advantage of shadows and covering brush as he quartered down the gentle slope toward the stables. Intent on reaching the mules and ponies, the Sioux didn't sight the hard running detail until Rick reached the broad circle of firelight.

Sioux horsemen, sighting the line of men, made a rush. They drove in to cut between Rick's detail and the stables. War arrows whizzed past. One red rider, hanging low from the back of his pony, let go with an old brass-bound trade musket.

"Yagh!" the warriors whooped. "Yagh!"

Rick turned his head and barked, "Halt! Face to your left! Commence firing!"

Sam, obeying, dropped to one knee, pitching the Springfield stock to his shoulder. He missed the Henry but it was good to feel the shock of the army gun against his shoulder as he aimed, then pulled the trigger.

Shorty knelt at his side. He hadn't fired. In the approved style of old Indian fighters, he waited for his partner to let go then fired while the friend reloaded. That way, Indians could not draw bullets then rush in and cut down opponents between volleys.

In the uncertain light Sam wasn't sure that he had hit a living target. But he grinned and calmly thrust a finger-long shell into his rifle chamber. Shorty was taking his time, getting the feel of the balance and hang of an unfamiliar weapon.

"The danged bay'nit," he said, from the corner of his mouth, "sorta pulls the front sight down. Out'n kilter. Man wants to allow for that."

Private Huffenberger, not yet a veteran, put his first bullet into the earth ten feet from where he was crouching. Rick Sling, ranging up and down his line, head and shoulders up, bent and patted the rookie on the shoulder as the sweating lad fumbled in reloading.

"Take it easy, son," he admonished. "We got all night to whip 'em. Get your sights in line. Hold and squeeze!"

"Ye—yes sir," stammered Huffenberger.

Spike Dillon, siding the recruit, fired slowly and calmly. A war arrow hit the earth directly to his front and hung there, its shaft quivering. Spike, shifting his aim, knocked the bowman off his pony.

Bootle leaped up, quavering. "I'm headin' for the stables! They'll ride over us here!"

Rick tried to slap Bootle down into line. "Keep your head down," he ordered.

Bootle broke away from the line, seeking to gain the shelter of the stable. He checked as though he had bumped into a rock. A war arrow caught him in the throat. He plunged forward with a clatter of belt and arms. Huffenberger, aiming, dropped his rifle point, gulped, turned his head aside and lost his supper.

Spike Dillon, reaching out, slapped him on the back. "That's right, lad," he said heartily. "Lighten yourself for the fight!"

"Cah!" panted Huffenberger. But he raised the Springfield with shaking hands and fired.

"Good!" yelled Dillon, telling a blessed white lie. "You knocked that big Sioux buck gallivantin'"

"Sure enough?" breathed Huffenberger.

"Sure as I'm a church member," said Spike.

Sam and Shorty saw Bootle die with the arrow in his throat. They exchanged not a word. They centered their gunfire on the riders who were striving to cut them off from the stable. Sam hit a pony. Shorty dropped a warrior. That took off the flank pressure.

"Now!" Rick yelled. "Make for the stable!"

They reached the lines and flopped down on the flank of a line of sweating and cursing soldiers and civilians.

"Gawd sakes!" cried old Shorty. "Red Dog and Jake! What you mule skinners doin' here?"

"Your pard, Tom, organized us to help you bust out'n the guard-house. But as we got set, the danged Sioux took the play away from us."

"Where's Tom?"

"Ain't seen him. Us boys busted down here to help out."

The Sioux had already reached some of the outside picket lines and stampeded the horses. But the frightened braying mules, hating Indian smell, had bunched up around the old gray bell mare. Wisps of hay, carried from the blazing stacks, now and then lit on a mule's nervous back, driving the beast to the point of madness from pain.

CHAPTER 22

The bulk of the mule herd was saved by a small force of experts including Jake and Red Dog. Sam went along with them. They led the bell mare into the pole corral. The mules, a good thirty head, trailed after her. At the gate of the corral, Sam encountered Lieutenant Prime. Fire and smoke and sweat had taken all the polish off his uniform. A slug from an Indian musket had broken his right arm between elbow and wrist. Prime was half mad with pain and vexation at the loss of his ponies. But he had fashioned a sling for his arm from his neck scarf and was wobbling around, keeping his men in line.

"Whole detail's here," he told Sam. "Ordered in from the trading post for remounts!"

"Who's guardin' the wagon train?"

"Plenty of teamsters there."

"But most of those mule skinners are here tonight." Sam didn't say that taking the guard off the train had been just another dumb army order. He surmised that Canada Pete had pulled the wool over Budhouse's eyes. Then it sank in on Sam that there were women with the unguarded train. Given this information, Prime became alarmed. "What'll become of Miss Payne?" he wanted to know. "What'll become of her?"

"I don't think the Sioux'll hit the post. That's Pete's

property. This is just a small force of Injuns sent in to bother the army so it won't keep an eye on Pete."

"We'll mount up on mules," said Prime. He shouted to the grimy stable sergeant to select some mules that had been broken to ride.

But Sam shook his head. The Indian attack was at its height. A group of riders could not break through.

"We can try it!" the lieutenant raged, and shouted for the saddling detail to hurry the work.

A knot of Sioux riders, angered that the mules had escaped them, rode down boldly. War arrows whizzed, clattering against the rails of the corral. Sam dropped to his knees, thrusting out an arm and attempting to pull down the lieutenant. Prime dropped but not through Sam's aid. An arrow snapped into his left shoulder. He was totally disabled. His six-shooter dropped from his hand as he fell and Sam scooped it up.

Sam called to a soldier dodging past him, his rifle cocked for a fast shot. "Take care of your loot. He's bad hurt. Put him in the shade."

Sam turned and crawled back to his place in the line. As he dropped down between Shorty and Red Dog, he heard his friends cursing. A bugle was blaring from brush down by the river.

"Some danged deserter," growled Red Dog. "I wish I could see him to shoot."

"No deserter," said Sam. "If you saw him, he'd be wearin' a blue coat. That's Pete."

"Pete?" cried Red Dog. "But he was in on the deal to help you get out. Him and Chicago Jack. Both of 'em orter to be here. Jack told us, after we got you and Shorty out, you'd show us a secret trail to Montany. If this Injun deal hadn't busted out, we'd be hookin' up now to start north."

So that was why Jack had wished to draw Sam into some sort of a deal. To act as a guide on another attempt to crack the army deadline.

The steady fire from the front of the corral turned back the Indian attack. The Sioux withdrew sullenly to the brush, uttering derisive yells as they rode off. But they would come again.

There ensued a space which didn't seem long to Sam, yet hours were speeding past. Men in the heat of battle seldom note the march of time. There were wounded men to care for, dead men to be dragged back and covered up with saddle blankets. Huffenberger counted himself an old soldier now. He had been nicked in the right leg with an arrow but Rick had cut it out. Huffenberger stayed on the line, saying that a man didn't need legs for shooting a rifle. Dillon was handling himself coolly, a tower of strength to recruits on the line in their first fight.

Jake, the mule skinner, had stopped a slug from an Indian musket with his hard head and gone silently to the Happy Hunting Ground of all good mule skinners.

Shorty, who had borrowed a plug of tobacco from Red Dog, would have enjoyed this fight if he could have located Tom Bear Mouth. But Tom was not to be found along the line.

Sam had felt assured that the train was not in immediate danger when he heard the bugle in the brush. So long as Canada Pete lingered near the post, driving on the warriors, Jane Payne and the other women would not be in danger.

Near midnight, the dirty, red-eyed stable sergeant broke out some rations of fat bacon and hard tack which his grimy followers wolfed down. The main attack had either been broken or the Sioux horsemen had withdrawn with the herd of ponies they had stolen. A few bold warriors still lingered in the river thickets, armed with trade muskets.

Sam and Shorty had decided that with the garrison

again in command of the situation, they would attempt to break through the lines. They would not trust to mules, but take the trail afoot. It was only a mile to the trading post. Sam retained Prime's pistol. He had not wasted any cartridges. He had depended upon the army rifle. Shorty borrowed a hand gun from Red Dog and a few rounds of extra ammunition.

They were talking over their plan for the break—neither called on any soldier for advice. A dim figure came weaving up from the river, half seen in the dancing light of the fire from the stacks which had now subsided to a red bed of glowing embers.

"An injun!" Red Dog said bitterly, firing.

The Indian came on. He began to yell. "Shoshone!" Shoshone!"

Shorty struck down the barrel of the mule skinner's gun. "That's Tom." he yelled. "He's hurt! Hold your fire!"

Shorty leaped like a rabbit from the line. He began to run toward his faltering partner, Sam close at his heels. They both saw the figure of a soldier also speeding toward the staggering Shoshone.

"Rick!" panted Sam.

Rick put his arm around the Indian, trying to help him in a run for the firing line. A gun boomed from the river. Rick slumped to the ground wounded.

Sam and Shorty brought in the wounded men. The firing line combed the brush with Springfield slugs.

Rick had been shot through the torso. Tom Bear Mouth carried a broken off war arrow in his right shoulder. Not a serious wound but long journey trailing had weakened the Shoshone, and the wound had sapped his strength. The farrier sergeant, who dealt with the diseases of horses and mules, tied up the hole in Rick and observed gruffly to Sam that he thought the old sergeant would make it. "He's tough," he said.

"Put him over here where the heat won't reach him."

They laid out Rick and Tom in the shadows. Prime was there, gritting his teeth against pain, striving to cheer up his disabled men. Sam bent over his brother while Shorty listened to Tom.

"Can you talk, Rick?" he asked.

"Sure, boy! Always good at talkin'." Rick smiled faintly. "What's on your mind?"

"Farrier sergeant says you'll make the grade, Rick. That—that was a danged brave thing you did. Savin' the life of an Injun."

"Injun," breathed Rick. "Well I'll be danged. I heard him yell for help and I went out for him." He grinned. "It might have been Huffenberger, you know."

"Rick, they'll take care of you now. I've got to go. With Shorty."

"Where, boy?"

"Canady Pete was here with the Sioux earlier. But I don't think he's around now. They've coaxed away all the civilians from the train. There's white women out there."

"And a Missoury cornfed," whispered Rick. He raised his right hand weakly. "Well, boy, this time I won't try to stop you from goin' over the hill."

Sam and Shorty slipped away from the corrals and the glowing coals that had once been stacks of hay. They worked their way, under the cold stars, up through the sagebrush to the low ridge above the cantonment. They lay for some time, listening. Below them an army gun fired now and then, the muzzle blast twinkling in the darkness like a glow worm. The bitter smoke of burnt powder and hay was heavy on the wind. But the fight had been waged. The Sioux, for the time, had been repulsed. Sam and Shorty saw, at the eastern limits of the camp, some red beds of embers where warriors had dashed in and set fire to a dozen tents of the doughboys.

"That old cap'tin," said Shorty, "will be lookin' things over and shapin' up for tomorrow's work."

"What did Tom say to you?" asked Sam. "About the Night Star."

"She's still alive and safe and hid out near the tradin' post. She promised Tom she wouldn't hurt herself." Shorty was musing. "You know, Sam, I'm kinda old like. But that Night Star needs somebody to help her out. If she's willing', I think I'll hunt up a black robe father and me and her will get hitched up legal. Then she can go with me and Tom to the Rockies."

"She needs kindness, Shorty. Let's hope we keep our hair on to reach the tradin' post."

But it required hours of careful scouting to slip through the night to their goal. They yearned to stand on their legs and run. But Sioux might be in camp any place along this ridge they were following. They held grimly to shadows and cover, depending on their rangecraft.

Dawn was breaking when they crawled down from the crest of the brushy hill that loomed to the rear of Pete's post. Their eager eyes checked on the buildings and the vehicles of the train. The place had not been attacked.

When they reached the trading post, Little Bird met them. They entered the cabin and found the Night Star bedded down on the dirt floor. Sunset Liz and her girls were ministering to the Indian woman whose eyes were bright with fever.

"Poor thing," said Sunset Liz. "But she'll live. She come down here to knife Canada Pete but he had already pulled out."

"Pulled out?" cried Sam. "When?"

"First crack of day. Half hour ago. They took that Missoury gal with 'em. Pete took her away from her guardeen at gun's point. Chicago Jack thinks Pete knows a secret trail to Montany. Since they had to travel fast and light, they only took my wagon." Liz curled a bitter lip. "My barrel of pain killer's in it."

Shorty, who had been roving around outside, came in. He had discovered blocks of ice and brush used for insulation around the ice house entrance.

"That's where Pete had his guns cached," said Sam. "Army searched and got down to the ice likely. Guns and ca'tridges hid under the ice. Safe even if the ice house caught fire."

Little Bird touched Sam on the arm. She drew him aside. "Pete like too many women," she said. "I show you trail. Old Sioux trail. He go to meet my brother."

"Who's your brother, Little Bird?"

"He wild boy. He called Kicking Horse."

"We'll take a couple of these mules, Little Bird. Pete won't be expectin' anybody to chase him so early."

Shorty wished to ride but Sam declared it was Shorty's duty to ride herd on the women in the trading post. Undoubtedly a relief party from the cantonment would soon arrive. But Pete had to be stopped, the Missouri girl rescued, and Kicking Horse prevented from receiving the renegade guns and shells.

Sam and Little Bird rode away from the post. The Indian woman wore a blanket draped around her ample figure. As the two jogged away, Sunset Liz called after them. "Sam, give a slug for me to Chicago Jack. He turned me down hard. And after you wipe him out, bust in the barrel of painkiller and see what he hid out. That's why he's do danged anxious to get to Montany."

Little Bird showed Sam the tracks of the broad-rimmed wheels of the wagon faintly appearing on the hard red shale of a dry stream bed. This was the start of a trail known only to the Sioux and renegades like Canada Pete.

CHAPTER 23

Through the craft of Little Bird, the pursuers overtook Pete and Chicago Jack in a rocky little draw where sagebrush grew high on the surrounding hills. Little Bird was in the lead. Wrapped in her blanket, she appeared to the white men like a messenger, guiding them to the place where the guns and cartridges would be turned over to Kicking Horse.

Chicago Jack was riding his pony alongside the lumbering wagon. Canada Pete was on the high seat, driving the four head of lumbering mules. Little Bird rode in from the flank, blanket fluttering in the wind. Her face was calm, inscrutable. Her appearance startled Pete. He slowed down his team and set his brake.

"Go on back," he ordered harshly. "You ain't wanted out here!"

Little Bird made no reply. She checked her mule. She waited while Sam Sling, with a drawn hand gun, called to Chicago Jack. "You wanted me in on this deal, Jack. Remember when we talked about it up the country?"

Jack cursed and spun his horse around to face Sam. He reached for his holstered gun but Sam's Colt was lined upon him.

"I didn't figure, Jack, that the deal we talked over

meant selling guns and shells to Sioux Injuns. Or runnin' off with white women."

Jack's face was contorted with rage. He watched Sam, waiting for a break.

"I don't know nothing about renegade guns," he said. "The wagon's loaded with flour and bales of beaver pelts. And a big barrel of painkiller. We aim to get to Montany, Sam."

"How about the Payne girl?"

Jack grinned wolfishly. "Maybe she yearned to come with us, Sam. She'a back there restin' soft on them beaver pelts."

"I know where Pete got those pelts," said Sam. "The pelts and the girl are coverin' up the rifles and shells he figures to deliver soon to Kicking Horse. And most likely, Jack, when he turns that trick you'll lose your hair."

Jack turned his head and called up to Pete, who sat on the wagon seat. "You didn't say nothing about guns, Pete. Are you double crossin' me?"

"So long, Jack," drawled Pete, and he whipped up a hand gun and shot Jack between the eyes. Jack reeled and fell from his pony. His left toe caught in the stirrup. The horse, alarmed by the bark of Pete's gun, stampeded, dragging the dead body after it.

Pete turned on Sam, swinging up the smoking gun.

"Your war medicine ain't strong enough, Sam," he started to say. He was smiling as though this meeting was all a huge joke.

Something whirred through the air. A war arrow drove throught the breast of Pete. His gun exploded. But his bullet was wild. His body twisted to the side, and dropped from the high seat to the earth.

Little Bird rode up. She carried a bow and stared down at Pete who lay on his back with the painted arrow shaft protruded from his body.

"He no good," Little Bird said. "Too many women." She touched her breast. "Me—I'm his wife!"

A girl screamed in the wagon. Sam found Jane Payne in the wagon box, tied up, laid out on bales of beaver pelts. Pelts that had once been on stretchers in the Big Horns. Beneath the girl and the pelts, Sam found several wooden cases containing magazine rifles and boxes of fixed ammunition.

He freed Jane. She was wide-eyed and afraid while he helped her from the wagon. She shuddered and turned her eyes from the form of Canada Pete. The Indian wife led her away from the wagon.

Sam's first thought was to turn the wagon and head back for the post. The mule teams had not stirred at the roll of gunfire, since Pete had set his brake before he killed his man.

Peering out the front of the wagon, from under the canvas top stretched over hickory hoops, he saw the horsemen in the distance, slipping down through the brush. Kicking Horse was coming for his guns.

He shouted to Jane to mount up on his mule and ride with Little Bird for the post. He didn't hear her answer. There was no time for talk if he prevented the Indians from seizing the guns and shells. He'd burn them, and throw on the blood-stained pelts to make a hotter hell fire. There'd be no chance to get away if he lingered here.

An axe was fastened to the back of the wagon seat. Sam took the axe and beat open the head of the big wooden barrel of painkiller. He tilted the barrel and let its contents gush over the stack of pelts, and the cased guns and cartridges beneath. When the barrel was empty, he recalled that Liz had told him that Jack had desired to get to Montana because of the barrel's contents. But surely one lone barrel of trade whiskey wouldn't induce a frontiersman to risk his scalp.

Sam wasn't amazed then when he drew two leather bags of gold coins from the barrel of painkiller. So Pete and Jack had been parts in the raid on the paymaster. Sam pitched the bags of coins from the wagon. If the army ever came up, they'd find some evidence that would clear old Rick of any involvement in the raid.

Then Sam took out a block of sulphur matches, struck one, and when it had taken on a good red glow, dropped it into the whiskey-soaked pile of pelts. Then he stepped down from the wagon, walked away a few paces, drew his hand gun, and prepared to meet the Sioux.

They were coming slowly. They were still a quarter mile distant when the fire in the wagon flared up. They made a nervous circle when the flames reached the boxes of cartridges and the shells began exploding.

Then they rode up, not on the run, but slowly. Sam met them. Jane Panye hadn't run away. Little Bird was there also, wrapped in her blanket, and standing unconcerned, over the sprawled body of Canada Pete.

Sam saw Kicking Horse. The war chief was burning with rage as he came riding on, leading a dozen of his warriors. With the party were old Sioux braves in blankets and paint and feathers.

Sam said softly to Jane Payne, while he watched the approaching Indians, "There's five live loads in this gun, Jane. Prime handed it to me."

"Good for the lieutenant." She was brave. "Save the last two loads, Sam."

"The first then for Kicking Horse. That one over there the pony painted on his brisket."

"I wish you could sing to me, Sam. Your buffalo song."

"I can't think of a good verse right now, Jane. But

you know what I'm thinkin'. Of all the little gals from old Missoury—"

"Cornfeds," she whispered.

He broke it off. The Sioux had halted. An old man came forward on a pacing pony. The old man carried an eagle plume fan and the tail of his eagle feather war bonnet reached to the top of the sagebrush. He averted his face from the heat of the huge bonfire that had once been a wagon load of guns, cartridges and beaver pelts.

Sam believed this was the end. The aged chief was pointing a long lance. Slowly he raised the pistol and aimed on to Kicking Horse.

Little Bird stepped aside, revealing the body of Canada Pete and the painted arrow shaft protruding from his body. She talked to the old chief with hand signs in the Sioux lingo. When she had finished, the old chief looked at Sam and the Missouri girl. Then he touched up his pony, rode over and spat down on the body of Pete.

"He no good," the chief said calmly.

Kicking Horse drove his pony forward. He saw Pete's body and the arrow in it. He checked his mount. Rage gripped him. But he turned aside when the old chief touched his pony on the withers with the eagle plume fan.

Without another word, the Sioux turned their horses slowly and rode off into the hills.

"And there," Sam said, "goes your Sioux war."

"What happened?" Jane whispered. She was weaving around on her legs now that danger had passed. Sam found it necessary to wrap his arms around her.

"That old chief," he said, "was the father of Kickin' Horse and Little Bird. He never was strong for any war. He had argued against it with other old men but Pete's guns was the ace in the hole of Kickin' Horse and the younger bucks. Pete got too prosperous when he tried to run out on a high born Sioux woman like Little Bird. She sure told her father plenty about him. And that was enough to show them that Pete had been bad medicine from the start for the Sioux."

The relief column under old Captain Budhouse rounded up the rags and tags of the fight with the Sioux from the raided cantonment to the post by late afternoon. He met Sam and Jane Payne and the recent widow of Canada Pete when they finally came into the post. He rode back with Sam to the scene of the burning of the wagon. The bags of gold were there, evidence clearing up the raid on the pay coach.

Private Huffenberger and Spike Dillon were in the detail, glad that at last they'd get paid off. Twisted metal parts of rifles were found in the charred ruins of the wagon, pinning down Canada Pete as a renegade. The marks in the arrow driven into his evil heart matched those on the broken bits of shaft which Rick had carried in his pocket.

Returning to the post, Captain Budhouse met a frightened girl.

"I suppose," she said to him, "you'll arrest Sam now for stealing your old horse."

Budhouse turned a grim eye on Sam and then he smiled. "I regret to tell you, Miss Payne, that Corporal Dillon will not sign an affidavit. He states under oath that he could not identify the man who stole his horse. So the army is forced to give a clearance to Sam Sling, and hereafter, ma'am, keep him to the straight and narrow and out of the guard-house. His brother's alive and will make the grade. He'd wish me to tell you that."

Shorty and Tom Bear Mouth rode slowly past the

trading post, pointing their ponies toward the west and the Continental Divide. The Night Star was with them, hiding her face in her blanket but riding straight in the saddle. The bad medicine man, who had betrayed her and her husband, was gone. Old Shorty would be kind to the grieving Night Star.

Little Bird, now sole proprietor of the post, was inside the cabin dealing out goods to mule skinners and soldiers liquid goods, for the men were singing. The soldiers had gold to spend.

"Sing us a farewell song, Sam," Shorty said.

Sam reached for the tough hand of his old partner.

"I can't sing," he said. "For once in my life, I can't sing, Shorty. But long life and good camps, old friends."

Before he rode on, Shorty took something off his saddle. He handed it down to Sam. It was a blue army blouse.

"We found it inside Pete's cabins," he said. "You can give it back to the good soldier who lost it. Your brother, Rick."

"What about the old bugle?"

"It never showed up. Maybe Pete lost it in the river fight. But wherever it is, you can bet Kicking Horse no longer figures it as good medicine."